The Valentine Mystery
by

Kathi Daley

I want to thank the very talented Jessica Fischer for the cover art.

I so appreciate Bruce Curran, who is always ready and willing to answer my cyber questions; Jayme Maness for helping out with the book clubs; and Peggy Hyndman for helping sleuth out those pesky typos.

And, of course, thanks to the readers and bloggers in my life, who make doing what I do possible.

Thank you to Randy Ladenheim-Gil for the editing.

And a special thanks to Nancy Farris, Taryn Lee, Janel Flynn, and Marie Rice for submitting recipes.

And finally I want to thank husband Ken for allowing me time to write by taking care of everything else.

Books by Kathi Daley

Come for the murder, stay for the romance.

Zoe Donovan Cozy Mystery:

Halloween Hijinks
The Trouble With Turkeys
Christmas Crazy
Cupid's Curse
Big Bunny Bump-off
Beach Blanket Barbie
Maui Madness
Derby Divas
Haunted Hamlet
Turkeys, Tuxes, and Tabbies
Christmas Cozy
Alaskan Alliance
Matrimony Meltdown
Soul Surrender
Heavenly Honeymoon
Hopscotch Homicide
Ghostly Graveyard
Santa Sleuth
Shamrock Shenanigans
Kitten Kaboodle
Costume Catastrophe
Candy Cane Caper
Holiday Hangover
Easter Escapade
Camp Carter
Trick or Treason
Reindeer Roundup

Hippity Hoppity Homicide – *March 2018*

Zimmerman Academy The New Normal
Ashton Falls Cozy Cookbook

Tj Jensen Paradise Lake Mysteries by Henery Press:

Pumpkins in Paradise
Snowmen in Paradise
Bikinis in Paradise
Christmas in Paradise
Puppies in Paradise
Halloween in Paradise
Treasure in Paradise
Fireworks in Paradise
Beaches in Paradise – *July 2018*

Whales and Tails Cozy Mystery:

Romeow and Juliet
The Mad Catter
Grimm's Furry Tail
Much Ado About Felines
Legend of Tabby Hollow
Cat of Christmas Past
A Tale of Two Tabbies
The Great Catsby
Count Catula
The Cat of Christmas Present
A Winter's Tail
The Taming of the Tabby
Frankencat
The Cat of Christmas Future
Farewell to Felines – *March 2018*

Writers' Retreat Southern Seashore Mystery:

First Case
Second Look
Third Strike
Fourth Victim
Fifth Night
Sixth Cabin – *May 2018*

Rescue Alaska Paranormal Mystery:

Finding Justice
Finding Answers – *May 2018*

A Tess and Tilly Mystery:

The Christmas Letter
The Valentine Mystery
The Mother's Day Mishap – *April 2018*

Sand and Sea Hawaiian Mystery:

Murder at Dolphin Bay
Murder at Sunrise Beach
Murder at the Witching Hour
Murder at Christmas
Murder at Turtle Cove
Murder at Water's Edge
Murder at Midnight

Seacliff High Mystery:
The Secret
The Curse
The Relic
The Conspiracy
The Grudge
The Shadow
The Haunting

Haunting By The Sea
Homecoming By The Sea – *April 2018*

Road to Christmas Romance:
Road to Christmas Past

Chapter 1

Wednesday, February 7

"Mornin', Tess, mornin', Tilly," Queenie Samuels greeted my dog Tilly and me. "It looks like a two-bagger today."

I groaned as I accepted two large mail bags from the postal employee who had recently been hired to help with mail distribution for the White Eagle, Montana, branch of the United States Postal Service. I supposed I should have anticipated the extra workload with Valentine's Day just around the corner.

"Your mom has a package requiring a signature," Queenie informed me. "If you want to sign it out, you can just drop it by her place with the mail to save her the trouble of coming in for it."

I accepted the clipboard and signed my name, Tess Thomas, in the spot reserved for a signature from my mother, Lucy Thomas. I had to admit I was curious about what was in the small box with the foreign postmark.

"The box came from Italy," Queenie informed me as I studied the postmark. "I'm not sure who Romero Montenegro is, but I do love the name. It's so strong and masculine; I can't help picturing a half-naked man with dark skin, chiseled features, and dark and soulful eyes every time the name Romero rolls off my tongue."

"You've definitely been reading too many romance novels."

"There's no such thing as reading too many romance novels." Queenie winked.

I opened the top of one of the bags and peered inside. "Did you happen to notice a box for my Aunt Ruthie while you were packing everything up?"

"There was a package. Flat and heavy. I'm thinking a book of some sort."

"It's a photo album. Her son Johnny just had a baby a few weeks ago and Ruthie has her first granddaughter. Johnny promised to send a photo album of baby's first week, and Ruthie has been asking about it every day since she spoke to him. She'll be thrilled it finally arrived." I glanced down at my golden retriever, Tilly. "Are you ready to get started?"

Tilly barked once in reply.

I thanked Queenie, and then Tilly and I headed out to my Jeep. Normally, I just parked on one end of Main Street and made my deliveries up one side and down the other. A two-bagger, however, required a slightly different approach; I parked in the middle of the long row of small mom-and-pop-type businesses with the intention of starting in the middle, working one side of the street, crossing, and then doing the other half of the north end, before returning to my Jeep for the second bag and repeating the effort on the south end. The diner my mom owned, along with my Aunt Ruthie, was close to the center of town, so I decided to park there and deliver their packages first.

"You're early today," Mom greeted as Tilly and I walked in through the front door at around the same time the breakfast crowd was beginning to disperse.

"Two-bagger."

"Ah. I guess that makes sense. Would you care for some coffee?"

"I don't have time to stay, but I did want to bring you this." I handed my mom the package from Italy.

She looked so completely shocked *and* so completely delighted when I handed it to her that I knew there had been more going on with the foreigner she had met briefly last summer than she was willing to let on.

"Isn't the package from the same man who sent you a card at Christmas?"

"Yes," Mom said, slipping the small package into the large pocket on the front of her apron. "As you know, we met when he was passing through last summer. Since then, we've exchanged correspondence. He's a very nice man I've enjoyed getting to know."

"Queenie said Romero Montenegro sounds like a name belonging to a muscular man with chiseled features and soulful eyes."

Mom quickly glanced away. She picked up a rag and began wiping an already clean counter.

"So, does he have soulful eyes?" I couldn't resist teasing the woman who, as far as I knew, had never even been on a date since she'd been informed my father died fourteen years ago.

"He's a very nice-looking man. Now, if you don't mind, I have customers to see to."

I looked around the half-empty restaurant. Everyone looked to be taken care of, but I didn't argue. I hated it when my brother, Mike, teased me about my love life, and I thought it was mean of me to tease Mom about hers. "Ruthie's photo album came. Is she in the kitchen?"

"She is. She'll be thrilled it's finally here." Mom hurried over to the kitchen door and pushed it open. "Ruthie, come on out," Mom called. "Tess is here, and she brought the photo album Johnny sent."

The next twenty minutes were taken up by Ruthie showing Mom and me, as well as every customer who hadn't managed to escape before she opened the book, photos of little Holly Ruth Turner. She really was cute, but the extra time spent at the diner meant I was going to have to hustle to get my two bags of mail delivered before the shops in the area closed for the day. It was winter in White Eagle, which meant that, except for a few of the restaurants and the bars, the shops in town locked their doors and rolled up the sidewalks by five o'clock.

I managed to make up some time with my next few stops. I tried to pause and chat with a handful of people each day, figuring if I mixed it up, I could maintain the relationships I'd built over time without taking a ridiculous amount of time to complete the route assigned to me. Of course, the one stop where I could never seem to get away with a drop and run was the Book Boutique, the bookstore my best friend, Bree Price, owned.

"Oh good, perfect timing," Bree said as I walked through the front door with a large stack of mail. "Wilma was just asking me about the Valentine's Day party Brady's throwing at the shelter."

I smiled at Wilma Cosgrove, White Eagle's new librarian and a fellow dog lover, who had been standing at the counter chatting with Bree. "What do you want to know?"

"I've been thinking of adopting a second dog. Sasha gets bored at home by herself all day, and unlike you, I'm not lucky enough to be able to bring her to work with me. How exactly does the party work?"

I set Bree's mail on the counter. "It's basically an adoption clinic, but Brady has arranged to use the high school's multipurpose room. He's going to decorate it with a Valentine theme and offer punch and cookies to those who show up. He plans to secure the exits other than the main entry, so the dogs and prospective owners can socialize in a casual atmosphere without having to worry about the animals getting out. He even plans to provide bean bag chairs for cuddling, balls for throwing, and toys for playing. He wants folks to relax with and really get to know the dogs available for adoption."

"It sounds like fun. The event is Saturday?"

"Ten to two," I confirmed.

"Great. I'll plan to attend. Right now, I should get going. The library opens in twenty minutes."

After Wilma left, Bree grabbed me by the arm. "Come with me. You have to see this."

I let Bree drag me down the hallway to her office. Tilly trailed along behind us. Sitting in the middle of Bree's desk was a beautiful bouquet of flowers. "Wow. That's some bouquet. Who's it from?"

Bree shrugged. "No idea. The delivery guy who brought it this morning said the flowers had been ordered and paid for by a source who wished to remain anonymous."

"Was there a card?"

"Just a small one that said, 'Happy Valentine's Day from a friend.' I love the mystery of an anonymous gift, but I'm dying to know who it's from. I've been racking my brain since it was delivered, but I can't think of a single person who would send such a wonderful bouquet."

Like Bree, I had no idea who would have sent the flowers, but I was grateful. Bree had been so depressed since her last boyfriend had been sent to prison after admitting to stealing an old man's life savings. It was good to see a smile on her face and a sparkle in her eye for the first time in weeks. "Maybe the flowers were sent by a customer? Or someone from book club?"

Bree tilted her head, causing her long blond hair to drape over her shoulder. "There are a couple of guys in book club who've asked me out, but I made it clear to each of them that I wasn't looking for a romantic entanglement at this point. I can't think of a single guy who would do something like this."

"I'm sure the flowers are just an icebreaker, and the man who sent them will follow up. In the meantime, enjoy the mystery."

Bree shrugged. "Yeah. I guess that makes sense. Are you coming to book club tonight?"

"If I can get the route done in time. I have a two-bagger today, so I'd best get going."

"Okay. Let me know if you aren't going to make it for some reason. Otherwise, I'll plan on you being there. If you want, we can get dinner after."

"I'd like that. I'll see you at six."

I left the bookstore and continued down the main street. I'd finished a quarter of the route and was nearing the halfway point, where I'd exchange my empty bag for the full one, when I got a text from Brady Baker, the new veterinarian in town. He asked if I had time to hand out some flyers for the Valentine party. I texted back that I had time to hand them out, but I didn't have time to pick them up. He texted that he would have Lilly meet me in midroute.

Lilly Long was Brady's new partner. She seemed to have been a good choice because she not only had been a practicing veterinarian for eight years, but she appeared to be a small-town girl at heart. She fit right in with the local crowd, which I knew was wonderful for Brady, but I wasn't sure how I felt about her living and working with White Eagle's most eligible bachelor. Brady and I were just friends, and he'd said on several occasions that he and Lilly were just friends as well, yet the thought of the two veterinarians spending so much time together caused a twinge of jealousy I couldn't rationally explain. I texted Brady again and informed him where I'd be, so Lilly could meet up with me. Then I slipped my phone into my pocket and continued on my route.

"Afternoon, Hap," I said to Hap Hollister as I entered his home and hardware store.

"Seems like you're late today," Hap said as I set his mail on the counter. When I only had one bag of mail to deliver, his store was one of my first deliveries.

"Double-bagger."

"I should have known. Lots of folks getting cards from their sweethearts, I imagine."

"Cards and packages. Have you decided what you're getting Hattie for Valentine's Day?"

Hattie Johnson was Hap's wife, or ex-wife, or something. To be honest, I wasn't sure exactly where they stood legally. What I did know was that Hap and Hattie used to be married, but they separated, or possibly divorced, a few years ago and moved into separate residences, but they continued to spend time together and went out on weekly dates.

"I'm struggling with that one a bit. We have our date night tonight. I'm hoping she'll drop a few hints as to what she'd like."

"Will you be taking her out on the big night?"

Hap frowned. "I'm not really clear on that. On one hand, our relationship agreement stipulates that Hattie will make dinner for me every Sunday, as well as on the seven major holidays, and in exchange, I'll take her on a proper date I plan and pay for every Wednesday and every other Saturday. The problem is, Valentine's Day is on Wednesday. Wednesday is my night to provide a date, but Valentine's Day is a holiday and therefore Hattie's day to cook for me."

"I guess you'll have to talk to her about it when you see her tonight."

"Yeah. I guess I will. By the way, I've been meaning to ask how Tang is doing. I miss the little guy now that he no longer does your route with you."

"He's doing well. I'll try to bring him by for a visit later in the week."

Tangletoe, or Tang for short, was an orange-and-white-striped kitten I found tangled up in some fishing wire just before Christmas. When I first found him, he was too young to be left alone, so Tilly carried Tang on the route with us in a backpack. When he got a bit bigger, I knew it would no longer work to bring him everywhere I went the way I brought Tilly, so I adopted a buddy for him, a beautiful longhair black kitten named Tinder. Tang and Tinder seemed quite happy staying behind and destroying my cabin while Tilly and I delivered the mail.

Lilly was just pulling up into the loading zone in front of Cartwright's Furniture as I approached with the mail. I took a small detour to greet her at her car. The pretty woman with long black hair and huge brown eyes rolled down the driver's side window and handed me a stack of pink and white posters advertising the adoption event on Saturday.

"Brady says thank you, as do I," Lilly said as I tucked the posters into my bag.

"Tilly and I are happy to help. It'll be wonderful to find homes for as many of the shelter residents as possible."

"I know you plan to show up early on Saturday." Lilly tucked a lock of her long hair behind one ear. "Do you think you'd have time to stop by the bakery on Saturday morning to pick up the cookies Brady ordered?"

"No problem at all. Did he order them from Hattie?"

Lilly nodded. "Five dozen heart-shaped sugar cookies with pink frosting. Hattie said she'd throw in a cooler of punch."

"Okay. I'll pick up the sweets and be at the high school by eight to help with the setup."

"Thanks, Tess. You're a peach."

Lilly rolled up her window and pulled into traffic while Tilly and I continued our route. By the time I'd delivered all the mail I'd been entrusted with for the day, it was almost five o'clock. I knew I'd have to hurry if I was going to make it home to change and drop off Tilly and make it back into town by six o'clock for book club. We'd had snow earlier in the week, so I couldn't drive too quickly; still, I pressed the speed limit just a bit so as not to be late. My cabin was located outside of town in a rural area off the highway. It's an old, dilapidated building on a large piece of land surrounded by forest that I wouldn't trade for anything. There are times during the winter when having such a long commute gets tiresome, but whenever I stand on my deck and listen to the sweet sound of nothing, I know I'm truly living in heaven.

I was just slowing down to navigate a tight curve when I heard a loud crash. I barely had time to apply my brakes when a deer ran onto the road ahead of me. I swerved to avoid hitting him, which caused me to fishtail before coming to a stop in the middle of the road. After taking a few deep breaths to calm my nerves, I slowly pulled onto the gravel shoulder, where a vehicle sat motionless. Based on the damage to the front end, the crash I'd heard must have been this vehicle hitting something just seconds before I arrived.

Chapter 2

"Stay here," I told Tilly before I climbed out of the Jeep and headed toward the car. "Are you okay?" I called to the man who was sitting in the front seat.

"I'm fine. My door is stuck. I can't get it open."

I looked at the front end of the vehicle. It was totally smashed, pushing everything else back and buckling the frame. "I'll try to get the back door open." It took some effort, but eventually I was able to open the door enough for the man to climb over the seat and squeeze through the rear door. Once he was safely on the road beside me, I glanced down the embankment, where I noticed a second vehicle resting against a tree. I jogged down as fast as I could travel in the deep snow. I could hear the man I'd just rescued on the road behind me.

"Are you okay?" I called to the second man after knocking on the driver's side window.

He didn't answer. I tried to open the door, but it was stuck. I could see blood on his head, which had run down his face to the front of his shirt. His body was slumped forward but was held in place by the seat belt. He didn't appear to be conscious.

"We need to get him out of there," I said to the man who had followed me down the hill.

He tried to open the door while I called 911.

"The door is too badly damaged to open," he said.

"Maybe we can break the back window and get him out that way," I suggested.

"We'll need something heavy to break to do that."

"Maybe we can find a large rock. My name is Tess, by the way."

"Coby. Do you have a tire iron in your Jeep?"

"Yeah, I do. That's a good idea. I'll get it." I ran back up the embankment. The tire iron was in a compartment in the cargo area of my vehicle. I offered Tilly a few words of comfort because she seemed to be pretty wound up, and then returned to where Coby was waiting.

"Okay, stand back." I watched as he used the tire iron to smash out the rear window. He cleared as much glass as possible, then used his jacket to cover any sharp edges that were left before climbing onto the trunk of the car and into the interior. He made his way to the front seat and checked the man's pulse.

"He has a pulse, but barely," Coby informed me. "We really should try to get him out of the car. The front is folded in such a way that his legs are trapped under the dash. If I can get some leverage, I might be able to use the tire iron to bend back the metal and free him."

"How can I help?" I asked.

"Do you have a blanket in your Jeep?"

"In the cargo area. My dog, Tilly, lies on it so it will have dog hair on it, but it's thick and heavy."

"Go and get it while I try to free his legs."

I ran up to the Jeep and once again offered words of encouragement to Tilly as I removed her blanket from the bed of the Jeep. Then I hurried back to the car, where Coby was working on the unconscious man.

"I got his legs free, but I lost his pulse. We need to get him out of here and administer CPR. I'm going to try to lift him up out of the seat. I need you to climb in and help me lower him into the backseat. Be careful of the glass."

I hopped up onto the trunk and entered the vehicle the way Coby had. Once he'd lifted the man over the seat and out the back window, we settled him onto the blanket. Coby felt for a pulse. When he couldn't find one, he began CPR. After several tense moments, Coby informed me that the man was breathing.

"I hope we didn't hurt him worse than he already was by moving him," I said.

"It's usually best not to move a trauma victim, but without CPR he would have died for sure. I don't think we can get him up the embankment without help."

"That should be here soon. In the meantime, I have a first aid kit in my glove box. We should try to stop the bleeding from the wound on his head." I returned to my Jeep for the third time and grabbed the small bag of medical supplies I carried with me. By the time I returned to where Coby was waiting with the trauma victim, my brother Mike had shown up with his partner, Frank. An ambulance arrived right behind them, relieving Coby and me of the responsibility of keeping the injured man alive. Once the paramedics had control of the situation, Mike told us to wait in my Jeep while they carried the man up to the road. Shortly after the ambulance sped away, a tow truck arrived. Coby assured Mike that he was fine and didn't need to go to the hospital. Mike took our statements and then I offered to drive Coby, whose last name I found out was Walters, into town.

"Do you have anything in the car you'd like to take with you? Luggage maybe?" I asked.

"Actually, I do." Coby headed to his car, popped the trunk, and removed two medium-sized bags.

"This is Tilly," I introduced him to my dog after he settled into the passenger seat of my Jeep. "Are you staying at the Inn?"

"Yes. The Inn at White Eagle."

"I know the owner. I'll call her to let her know you're on your way."

"I'll need a rental car. Is there somewhere in town to get one?" Coby asked.

"Brad Mulligan owns the only gas station and repair shop in town. He has a few cars he rents out to his customers. I'll take you over to his place."

"I'm glad you and Tilly happened along when you did," Coby said after we were underway. Tilly had stuck her head in through the opening between the two front seats and offered our guest a warm doggy kiss in greeting. "Talk about an unanticipated turn of events."

"Everything seems to have happened rather quickly," I agreed. "The tall officer with the dark hair is my brother. I'm sure he'll want to speak to both of us again. Probably tomorrow. Had you planned to be in town long?"

"I'm doing some research in the area, so my stay is somewhat open-ended. Ms. Rosenberg from the Inn assured me this is a slow time of year for her, so I can stay as long as I need."

"Things won't pick up until June, so I think you're safe."

Our conversation paused as I pulled into the gas station. I got out and introduced Coby to Brad. Once it was clear he'd be able to supply Coby with a car, I gave him my phone number and headed home. By the time I got there, it was after seven-thirty. I texted Bree to apologize for missing yet another book club, then started the fire and fed all three animals. Once they were settled, I headed into my bedroom to change into warm, dry clothes.

I'd just returned downstairs when my phone rang. It was Coby.

"Did you get settled in at the Inn?" I asked.

"I did. I just wanted to thank you again. I don't know what I would have done if you hadn't happened to be following me."

"It's not a problem at all. I'm glad you weren't injured."

"The accident did some damage to my car, but I was wearing my seat belt, so I'm fine. If you hadn't been there, though, I'm not sure how long I would have been stuck in the damaged vehicle. I really am grateful, and I'd love to take you to lunch tomorrow as a thank-you for helping me out."

I hesitated before I answered. "As a mail carrier, I don't always have time for lunch, but I could either meet you before my shift for an early breakfast or after it for an early dinner."

"Breakfast would be great. Can you recommend somewhere?"

"My mom owns a diner in town, Sisters'. Would seven-thirty work for you?"

"Seven-thirty would be great. I'll see you then."

I hung up, then went into the kitchen to scrounge around for something to eat. I'd settled on a bowl of Cheerios with half a banana when my phone rang for the second time since I'd been home. It was Bree, wanting all the details. By the time I'd finished talking to her, I decided to skip dinner and go straight to dessert, so I grabbed a pint of ice cream from the freezer and settled in front of my computer. I had a bunch of emails, mostly junk, but there was one from my friend Tony Marconi marked "important." Tony was a genius who lived on a private lake about twenty miles from White Eagle. He was the sort who rarely called but often texted. The fact that he'd sent an email intrigued me. I opened it to find a photo of the interior of a convenience store. Behind the counter was a tall, skinny man with long, dark hair, a woman with a child of around five or six paying for a carton of milk and a box of doughnuts, and an older gentleman standing off to the side. The latter was out of the line of sight of the camera but clearly visible in the security mirror.

"Oh my God," I gasped as I studied the man reflected in the mirror. I picked up my phone and called Tony.

"Did you get it?" he asked.

"I just got home and saw the email. Where did you get the photo?"

"I found it by running the photo I showed you at Christmastime through my facial recognition software. It's only two years old."

I placed a hand on my chest as my heart began pounding. It felt like I was having a heart attack. My father had been a long-haul trucker who'd died in a fiery crash when I was fourteen. I always suspected there was something odd about his death, so I'd asked Tony to look in to it for me. It had taken him a decade to catch his first real break, a photo of my dad taken three years after he'd supposedly died, which had confirmed to me that things hadn't been as cut-and-dried as everyone seemed to want it to be. I'd asked Tony to keep looking, never suspecting he'd find something new less than two months after that first clue.

"Where was it taken?" I asked.

"A minimart just outside Gallup, New Mexico. I already checked with the store. No one there knew your dad, so I doubt he lives in the area. The store is attached to a truck stop. A lot of folks stop in on their way down the highway."

"Okay, better question: Who took the photo and why?"

"That is a better question," Tony agreed. "At this point I don't know. The photo was selected by my software, but when I tried to trace the origin of the file it came back as unknown. I'll keep working on it."

"Two years. Wow. This whole thing is so surreal. I can't believe my father has been alive all this time but has allowed Mom, Mike, and me, to think he's dead."

"I warned you when we started this that you might not like what we found."

I took a deep breath. "I know. I realize that at some point I'll probably end up wishing we'd just left things alone, but I have to know."

"Okay, I'll keep digging."

"Thanks." An image of my mother's expression of delight when I'd given her the gift from her Italian friend flashed into my mind. "If my father is alive, as it seems he very well might be, does that mean he's still married to my mother?"

Tony didn't answer right away. "I supposed he could be. Your mother thought your father was dead, so it's not like she took any steps to dissolve the marriage. Although she's in possession of a death certificate, so it could be possible the marriage was nullified when he was declared dead. If we want to know for sure, we'll need to talk to an attorney."

"Yeah, I guess that would be the best way to know how the law works in a situation like this."

"Is there a reason you want to know whether your parents are still married?"

"My mom has a new friend. A male friend," I specified. "He lives in Italy, so I doubt anything will ever come from their flirtation. I just wondered."

"If we prove your father is alive, we'll need to consider having a conversation with Mike and your mother. In the meantime, I think it's best to keep this just between us. Just because we have a photo of a man who looks so much like your father that the facial recognition software identified him as being Grant Thomas doesn't mean that's definitely who he is. We'd need DNA evidence or fingerprints to know for certain."

I picked up Tinder, who had wandered over to where I was sitting. "I agree it's best to keep this between us for now. We still have no idea why my dad would fake his death. However this turns out, I appreciate all the work you've put into it."

"I don't mind at all. It gives us a reason to get together, and you know how much I enjoy spending time with you and Tilly."

"I do. How's Titan doing? I've been meaning to bring Tilly by for a visit." Titan was a rescue dog I'd adopted for Tony last Christmas, after I'd found out the shepherd mix was alone in the world since his owner died. Tony was a bit of a loner who chose to live by himself in a mansion up on the mountain, but he seemed to adore Titan, who likewise adored his new dad.

"Titan and I are fine, but I know he misses Tilly. Do you want to come over tomorrow after work? I'll make you dinner and we can try out the video game I'm testing."

"Sounds wonderful. I might need to go talk with Mike about an accident I witnessed, but if not, I can be there by six."

"You witnessed an accident?"

"On my way home. I never did find out the name of the man who was taken to the hospital, but the other man is named Coby Walters. He said he's in town to do some research. I didn't ask him what he was researching, but I'm having breakfast with him tomorrow, so I'll see if I can find out then."

"Do you think it's a good idea to have breakfast with a total stranger?"

"Relax, Mom," I teased. "We're going to Sisters', so I'll have a lot of chaperones. I was going to make an excuse not to go when he first asked me, but now that I think about it, I'm sort of interested in what he's here to look in to. I'll tell you all about it tomorrow at dinner."

After I hung up, I studied the photo Tony had sent me. My dad had been away from home most of the time when I was growing up, leaving me feeling unloved and deserted. To make myself feel better, I'd begun to imagine he hadn't abandoned me to deliver canned goods from one coast to the other, but rather was some superimportant spy or superhero, ensuring the safety of all humankind. Pretending gave me comfort, so when I'd found a letter I was sure was a secret message, I'd taken it to Tony to decipher. Tony had assured me it was just a letter, not a code, but I was still obsessed with finding out who my father was and whether he was really dead. The remains that had been delivered to my mother had consisted of little more than ash, so as far as I was concerned, unless I could prove otherwise, Dad was both alive *and* dead. Tony had been drawn by my story and agreed to help me. He'd basically gotten nowhere until he'd found the ten-year-old photo of my dad standing in front of a building in Los Angeles. Tony had warned me that my dad might not be the good guy I imagined, and that digging into his disappearance when he seemed to have wanted to exit my life might not provide me with an explanation I could live with, but still, I had to know.

I logged off the computer, grabbed Tang and Tinder, called to Tilly, and headed to bed. It had been a long day, and tomorrow looked to be an even longer one. I needed to try to sleep despite the scenarios playing again and again in my mind. I don't know why I'm so obsessed with learning the truth, why I'd never accepted my father's death when both my mom and Mike seemed to have. It was almost like I knew something I couldn't quite bring into my consciousness but couldn't quite let it go.

Chapter 3

Thursday, February 8

Coby arrived at Sisters' just as I pulled into a parking spot. I got out, greeted him, and introduced him to Mom and Aunt Ruthie as soon as we entered the warm, homey restaurant. I had Tilly with me, so I grabbed a large booth toward the back of the dining room, where Tilly would be out of the way.

"Thank you for meeting me so early," I started. "Sometimes it works to take a lunch, but this week has been busy with the holiday."

Coby smiled. "I totally understand. I've already told you how grateful I am that you were there to help me last night and wanted to take you out for a meal as a thank-you."

"How are you liking White Eagle so far?" I asked as I stirred cream into my coffee.

"I haven't had a lot of time to look around, but I like what I've seen. I love the feel of small towns. Everyone I've met so far has been friendly and helpful."

"You said you were in town to do research. Are you a writer?"

"No. The research is personal in nature."

"I see." I didn't really and wanted to know what personal research Coby was in town to carry out, but asking would make me seem too forward, "I was born in White Eagle and have lived here my whole life. I'm happy to help if you need a local perspective."

Coby pulled a photo from his pocket and passed it across the table. "What do you see?" he asked as I took it from his outstretched hand.

"A very beautiful pregnant woman holding a blanket while standing in front of the old Honeycutt house."

"You know the place?" Coby asked. I couldn't help but notice the excitement in his voice.

"Sure. It's a big house just outside of town. Edith Honeycutt lived there until she died five or six years ago. It's been empty ever since. Did you know Edith?"

Coby shook his head. "It's kind of a long story and I know you have to get to work, so I'll see if I can condense it. I was adopted. I never knew who my real parents were and never really wondered about them until a few months ago, when my father died after a short illness. My parents were in their late forties when I was adopted. Both sets of grandparents were dead and I never had siblings, so I didn't have any extended family to speak of. My mom died when I was in high school, so it was just Dad and me for quite some time. He felt bad I was going to be left alone in the world, so on the day before he passed, he gave me this photo. He told me that he and Mom had adopted me through the foster care system, where I'd been ever since I was found in a church in Kalispell just days after I was born. I was wrapped in a blanket, and that photo was tucked in with me. My dad suspected the photo was of my biological mother, although he didn't know it for certain. On the back of the photo were the words, 'Where you go, so goes my heart.'"

"That's so sad. Are you here to try to track down the woman in the photo?"

Coby took a sip of his coffee. "If I can. I started my search in Kalispell by visiting the church where I'd been left on Valentine's Day thirty-four years ago. The pastor at that time passed away more than a decade ago, and the new one didn't know anything about me or where I might have come from. I spent some time speaking to parishioners who'd been around back then, but no one said they recognized the woman in the photo. A woman did recognize the blanket, however. Sewn into the corner is a logo with a small cat and the letters *CM*. The woman told me there used to be a gift shop in White Eagle called The Cat's Meow. The owner liked to knit and sold her own handcrafted wares in her store. The woman in Kalispell recognized the logo, so here I am. I figured I'd spend some time in town to see if anyone recognizes the woman in the photo."

"I'm only twenty-eight, so I wasn't born yet thirty-four years ago, but my mom and Aunt Ruthie both lived here then. We can ask them."

"That'd be great. Thanks."

I raised my hand and waved my mother over. When she arrived at our table I briefly explained what Coby was in town to accomplish. She looked at the photo but didn't recognize the woman. Like me, she recognized the house in the background, and she remembered The Cat's Meow, but the owner, Gilda Swan, had moved on quite a while back and she didn't know what had become of her. Aunt Ruthie said the same thing, but she offered to make a couple of copies of the photo, and I said I'd take one of them with me on my route. Mom and Ruthie promised to show the other to any longtime locals who stopped by for a bite to eat. They took Coby's cell number and one of us would call him if we found anything at all that might help him with his search.

After breakfast, I headed to the post office to pick up my mailbags and Coby went back to the Inn.

Trying to find a woman with only a single photo wasn't going to be easy, especially because she may only have been passing through town. Still, I wasn't a stranger to the pull of a mystery surrounding a parent, no matter how hopeless the quest might seem. Until Tony found that first photo at Christmas, I'd had a lot less than Coby to go on, and yet I had stuck with my desire to find out the truth about my dad for fourteen long years. Coby had only been looking a few weeks. Perhaps he'd find what he was looking for.

By the time I got to Bree's bookstore, it was well in to the afternoon. She was ringing up a customer when I arrived, but she signaled for me to wait rather than just dropping her mail and leaving, as I'd planned. I had a lot of territory to cover in a short amount of time if I was going to be done with my route by five, but Bree was my best friend, so if she wanted me to wait, I would.

"I received another gift," Bree said with a huge grin on her face the moment the customer left.

"More flowers?"

"Better." Bree set a box of chocolates on the counter. "They're really good. Have one, if you want."

I looked in the box and selected one I thought might have a caramel center. "Still no idea who the gifts are from?"

Bree shook her head as I took a bite of the dark chocolate. "Not a clue. I set my bouquet on the counter during book club last night. I hoped if it had been sent by someone in the group, they would say something or give themselves away in some way, but while everyone commented on how beautiful it was, no one said they'd sent it."

"Did you check with the florist and the candy shop to see who ordered the items delivered to you?" I selected a second piece of candy, then put the lid back on the box so I wouldn't end up eating Bree's entire gift.

She nodded. "All either merchant will say is that the sender wanted to remain anonymous."

I took Bree's hand in mine and gave it a squeeze. "I think you should just enjoy the gifts. It's so wonderful to see a smile on your face again."

Bree's smile faded just a bit. "I guess I have been sort of down in the dumps since Donny."

"You've gone through something really difficult, and it's understandable you'd feel a little down. But you seem happy now. Embrace the fun of the mystery."

"I guess, but I'd like to know who to thank."

"If the person wanted thanks, they would have included their name," I pointed out. "Enjoy the gifts and don't worry about who sent them."

Bree frowned at me. "It wasn't you, was it?"

"Sorry, no. If I knew that receiving anonymous gifts would help you out of your funk and had thought of it first, I might have done exactly what your anonymous friend has, but I didn't, so I can't take the credit." I glanced at the clock on the wall. "Listen, I have to go. We'll catch up later."

"Dinner?"

"I'm going over to Tony's tonight. How about tomorrow? We can try that new Italian place everyone is raving about. My treat."

"Okay, that sounds good. I'll text you tomorrow to work out the details."

I'd hoped to have time to show Coby's photo around, but I was behind on my schedule and I still had posters to hand out for Brady, so I decided that, except for Hap, the person I considered most likely to have known the woman in the photo, I'd wait to ask around more widely until the following day.

I intentionally left the part of town where Hap had his store until last so I could stop and chat for a minute. When I arrived, it was already a quarter to five and Hap closed at five in the winter, so our chat would have to be brief.

"I wondered what happened to you today," Hap said as Tilly and I walked in. "In fact, I'd all but decided I didn't have mail today."

"You have mail." I held up the small pile of envelopes before handing them to the tall, thin, white-haired man. "I was running behind and needed to talk to you, so I left you for last. I should have texted so you wouldn't worry."

"A text would have been nice."

"I know. I'm sorry." I leaned on the counter while Tilly went to stretch out by the fire. It had been a cold day and I could see she was anxious to settle in for the evening. Of course, I'd promised Tony I'd have dinner with him, but Tilly loved Tony and Titan, so my guess was she'd be fine with another trip out.

"What did you want to talk to me about?" Hap asked.

I handed him the photo. "Do you recognize this woman?"

He studied the photo. "No, I don't think so; at least nothing comes to mind. Who is it?"

I briefly explained Coby's reason for being in town. Hap took a second look at the photo, tilting his head from one side to the other as he thought. "You know, you might want to talk to Dotty Norris. She's lived just down the road from the Honeycutt house for close to fifty years. I remember Dotty and Edith being friends. Seems to me if Edith had a guest staying with her thirty-four years ago, chances are Dotty would be one of the few to remember."

"Thanks, Hap. I'll chat with Dotty tomorrow. Right now, I need to run. Tilly and I are supposed to be having dinner with Tony and Titan tonight."

"How's that boy doing? He used to stop by now and then, but I don't think I've seen him since before Christmas."

"He's been working on some secret project for whoever he works for. I have no idea exactly what it is, but it seems to be taking a lot of his time. I know he was out of town for two weeks last month because

Titan stayed with me while he was away, but I think he's about done at this point. I'll tell him to stop in and say hi when he's next in town."

"Do that. I always enjoy chatting with the lad."

I wouldn't exactly call Tony a lad. Not only was he twenty-eight and an adult by anyone's standards, but he was a good six feet four, with broad shoulders and a muscular build. The term *lad*, in my mind, conjured up someone young and scrawny, and Tony was neither. Of course, I suppose age is relative. To someone Hap's age, those of us who haven't yet reached thirty probably did seem like kids.

I'd just reached my Jeep when Mike texted me to ask if I could come to his office before heading home for the day. He was only a couple of blocks away, so I started my Jeep and drove in that direction. I parked in front, then sent a quick text to Tony, letting him know I might be a few minutes late. Then Tilly and I headed into Mike's office.

"You wanted to speak to me?" I said, sitting down across his desk. It was a mess and looked like he'd been sorting through old files.

"I just have a few questions about yesterday's accident," Mike said, shoving a pile of manila folders aside.

"Okay, shoot. What do you want to know?"

"You said last night that you were nearing the section of highway with that series of sharp curves when you heard a crash."

"That's correct."

"Did you actually see the accident occur?"

"No. I was still on the north side of the curves. I heard the crash and then a deer ran into the road. I swerved to avoid hitting him and momentarily lost control of the Jeep. By the time I regained it and managed to stop the Jeep, both vehicles were already where you found them."

"And both men were still in their cars at that point?"

"Correct. I approached Coby's vehicle first because it was still on the road. He was sitting in the driver's seat and appeared unharmed, but he couldn't get his car door open. I managed to force the back door open, which is how he got out. Once Coby was safely out of his vehicle, he and I went to check on the other man, who was unconscious. By the way, how is he?"

"I'm afraid he didn't make it."

"Oh, no. I'm so sorry."

"I only have a preliminary report to work off, but it looks like the cause of death was heart failure. I'm operating under the assumption he had a heart attack."

"Coby said the man's heart wasn't beating when he checked shortly after the accident. He administered CPR and his heart started beating again."

"When I spoke to Walters last night, he said he was following the vehicle driven by the other accident victim when the car spun out of control. He told me that he tried to avoid a collision but was unsuccessful. It appears the car Walters was driving hit the back of the car in front of him, pushing it off the road, where it traveled down the embankment and smashed headfirst into a large tree. I've gone back to the site and looked around, and it seems that for the lead car to hit the tree as hard as it did, the force to the rear of the vehicle had to have been significant. Walters swore he wasn't speeding, but I don't see how he couldn't have been. Did you see anything that might explain what caused that first vehicle to hit the tree at the speed it did?"

"The accident was over before I arrived. I guess if the man spun out of control and Coby ran into him, the force created by the two cars colliding could have caused the first vehicle to veer off the road at a significant rate of speed."

"Maybe."

I could tell by his expression that Mike still didn't believe things had gone down the way Coby said they had, but he was going to let it go for now.

"Were you able to identify the man who died?" I asked.

"According to his ID, his name was Armand Kowalski. His driver's license was issued in California and his home address is in San Francisco. I don't know a lot about him and I'm still trying to track down his next of kin. I have some feelers out, so I should know more by tomorrow. In the meantime, if you think of anything at all you want to add to your statement, give me a call."

Chapter 4

By the time I went home, changed my clothes, grabbed food for Tilly and both kittens, and drove us all up the mountain to Tony's, it was close to six-forty.

"Sorry I'm late," I said as I let myself and the animals in the front door. I let Tang and Tinder out of their car carrier while Tilly enthusiastically greeted Titan.

"I figured you might be after you texted, so I planned for dinner to be ready at seven. Would you care for a glass of wine or maybe a beer while we wait for the lasagna to be done?" Tony took my coat, hat, and mittens and hung them on the coatrack near the door.

"A beer would be great. Thanks." I followed Tony, who was dressed in faded jeans and a sky-blue sweater, into the kitchen. "It smells wonderful in here. I never had time to stop for lunch, so I'm starving."

Tony handed me a slice from the loaf of freshly baked French bread he had cooling on the counter. "You shouldn't go all day without eating."

"I didn't." I took a bite of the bread after spreading a pat of butter over it. "Remember, I had breakfast with Coby."

"That's right. How did that go?"

I briefly explained why Coby was in White Eagle. "Maybe you can use your facial recognition software to find the woman in the photo."

"I'd be happy to try if your friend wants me to. I think we should ask him first."

"I'll ask him tomorrow." I took another bite of the bread. It really was delicious. Soft and hot on the inside and crisp and browned around the edges. "It seems like forever since we've hung out. Did you finish the project you've been working on?"

"Yes, I did. I have another one I've been putting off until after I completed this one, but I think I'll take a few days off before I jump in. Did you finish your kitchen? The last time I spoke to you, you said you wanted to paint it."

"I never even started. Between working Monday through Friday, volunteering at the animal shelter on Saturdays, and keeping my mom happy by spending most Sundays with her, I haven't had any time to myself. I'm looking forward to hanging out and playing video games this evening. It's been a while."

Tony used a finger to wipe a smear of butter from the corner of my mouth. "It has. I've missed you. And Titan hasn't been happy that Tilly hasn't been coming around."

I glanced toward the fireplace. The two dogs were curled up, cuddling. They really did seem to love each other. "I need to make more of an effort to bring her by. Maybe Sunday. I've had dinner with my mom five weeks in a row. I think it's time I took a day for myself."

Tony smiled. "Sunday would be great. We can do anything you like."

A feeling of contentment washed over me as he removed the lasagna from the oven before sliding in the garlic bread in its place. Tang and Tinder had decided to join the dogs, and all four animals slept while Tony and I ate. I wanted to ask him about his research into my dad's whereabouts, but I hated to ruin the perfection of the evening, so I decided I'd wait to bring it up until after I annihilated him in whatever video game he'd agreed to test.

"What's going on with Shaggy?" I asked after we'd polished off an impressive amount of the lasagna. Shaggy, whose real name was Stuart, owned a video store in town and was Tony's best friend.

"Not a lot, as far as I know. I've been so busy, we haven't hung out much, but I do know he's working on a new distribution contract he thinks will help his business get the jump start it needs. In fact, I think he's in Denver this week."

"He's out of town?"

"As far as I know, he left a week or so ago. He said he was going to close the store for a couple of weeks so he could head out and visit his brother as long as he was going to be in Colorado."

"Dang, there goes my number one suspect."

"Suspect?" Tony raised a brow.

"Bree has a secret admirer who's been sending her gifts the past couple of days. I thought it might be Shaggy."

Tony looked surprised. "Why would he be sending Bree gifts? They barely get along."

"I know they fight a lot, but I sort of get the idea Shaggy's in to Bree, and teasing her is some sort of courtship ritual."

Tony lifted a shoulder. "I guess you have a point. It *is* odd how he picks on her more than anyone else. Still, I don't think he's the type to do something as subtle as send anonymous gifts. Jumping out at her with a can of Silly String is more his style."

"I guess you're right." I picked up my plate and took it to the sink.

"I'll get this stuff," Tony said.

"Okay, then I'll take the dogs out for a quick break while you clean up. I'd hate to be interrupted once the annihilation begins."

"Oh, I don't know." Tony winked. "I don't figure it will take me long to have you crying for mercy."

"We'll see who ends up doing the begging," I challenged as I called Tilly and Titan to my side and headed for the door. Tony and I both knew he could beat me at any game the industry had to offer, but occasionally he'd skillfully let me win without making it obvious he was doing so. In the beginning, I believed I'd beaten him, but after spending a considerable amount of time with him, I'd begun to pick up some very subtle tells when he was holding back.

It was a cold but clear night, and the dogs and I headed to the private lake on Tony's property. I wasn't sure exactly how much acreage he owned, but I knew he didn't have any neighbors for as far as the eye could see. I used to wonder why Tony would choose to live in such isolation, but the more time I spent with him, the clearer it became that he lived such a busy, challenging, intellectual life that the quiet was welcome during his downtime.

I was about to head back to the house when I received a text from Coby letting me know he might have found a lead and wondering if I'd be available to have breakfast again to discuss it. I texted back that I'd be happy to meet him at Sisters' Diner at the same time tomorrow morning. His mystery had intrigued me, and I was glad he was willing to let me join in on the search. I couldn't imagine why a woman would leave her newborn at a church, but my gut told me that Coby's mother must have had a good reason for doing it. I pulled out the photo I still carried in my pocket. The woman was beautiful, but her long dark hair and welcoming smile couldn't mask the haunted eyes that seemed to be looking at someone or something behind the photographer.

When the dogs and I returned to the house, the dishwasher was running and Tony was putting another log on the fire. "Before we get into our quest for world domination, I wanted to ask if there's anything about the search for my father you haven't already told me."

Tony took my hand and led me to the sofa. He indicated that we should take a seat. "So far, the only clues I have are the two photos I found. I'll keep looking, but I think we should be cautious as we proceed. I'm not thrilled that the photos aren't traceable."

"What do you mean by that?" I asked.

"Normally, the photos I find with my software can be traced back to an origination point. Some were initially posted on social media, or maybe they appeared with a news article. Other photos come from security or traffic cameras, while others are associated with drivers' licenses or some other type of identification. When I tried to run a trace on those photos, I got nothing. Obviously, someone took the photos and uploaded them to a location accessible via the internet, but the source has been masked. I think we're looking at some extremely high-level security."

"Like the CIA?"

Tony shrugged. "Maybe. Although there are other options. I think we need to proceed with caution so we don't tip off the wrong people that we're looking in the first place."

"What do you mean by the wrong people?" I couldn't keep the fear that had crept into my heart from my voice.

"If someone went to all the trouble to apply that much effort to mask the origination of the photos, they may also have set up an alarm letting them know if they were accessed. I'm not saying they'll be able to track my activity to your father—I have my own search security in place—but I feel like we're dealing with professionals who know how to play the game."

"Do you think my dad is mixed up in something dangerous or illegal?"

"I don't know, but we should keep that possibility in mind."

I sat back against the sofa but didn't reply. I hated the idea that the man who used to give me piggyback rides might have disappeared from our lives because he was a criminal who'd escaped some law enforcement agency. Of course, being a fugitive isn't the only reason a person might disappear. He could have been living a second life with another family and maybe the duplicity caught up with him. Or maybe he really was a spy or secret agent who'd removed himself from our lives to protect us.

"So, are you ready to try for world domination?" Tony asked.

"I was born ready," I teased as he booted up the game. "I'll need to keep an eye on the clock, however. I have another early morning and long day tomorrow."

"I guess I should have brought the game to you so you wouldn't have to drive home at the end of the evening."

"Next time for sure." I logged on to the game so my stats could be recorded. The first space robots had just shown up on the screen when my phone rang. I'd just entered the battle, so I let the call go to voice mail. When we came to a place it would be easy to pause the game, I asked Tony to do so. The call had been from Mike, and my smile turned to a frown as I listened to the message.

"Is there a problem?" Tony asked after I hung up.

"Mike had the crime scene guys search Armand Kowalski's car after it was towed to the impound lot. They found a photo of Coby in the glove box."

"So he knew Coby?"

"I'm not sure. Coby didn't say anything that would indicate he knew the man in the other vehicle last evening, and Mike said in the voice mail he'd called him in and showed him the photo. Apparently, it was taken while Coby was in Kalispell prior to coming to White Eagle, though he wasn't aware anyone had taken it and had no idea why the man would have it. Coby said he'd never seen or met him."

"What exactly did Coby tell you happened last night?" Tony asked.

"That he was following the other car when it spun out of control. He tried to avoid hitting it but was unable to do so."

"And the damage to the cars? Where was each car impacted?"

"Both had damage to the front end and Kowalski's car had damage to the rear. Coby said he hit the car in front of him after the driver lost control and spun around, but the front of Coby's vehicle hit the back of Kowalski's, so it must have turned all the way around. After Coby hit it, Kowalski's car plunged over the embankment and hit a tree, which must be what caused the damage to the front. I'm going to return Mike's call. Maybe he knows more than he said in the message."

"I'll grab us more beer," Tony offered.

"Just soda for me. I still have to drive home." I set my controller on the table in front of me and called Mike. He didn't pick up, so I left a message. Tinder settled into my lap and I put my hand to my mouth as I let out a long yawn. "Sorry. I guess I'm more tired than I realized."

"I understand," Tony said as he returned to the room with two sodas. "You've had a busy day. Maybe we should try the game another night."

"Yeah," I agreed. 'That might be a good idea. I'll call you tomorrow to let you know whether Coby wants you to use your facial recognition software on his photo."

"Okay, but be careful. Something about this thing doesn't feel quite right."

"Yeah." I said as I stood up and began to gather my things. "I've had the same feeling, but I can't put my finger on exactly what's bothering me. Maybe it'll come to me after I get some shut-eye."

Chapter 5

Friday, February 9

When I arrived at Sisters' Diner the next morning, Coby was already seated in what was becoming our regular seat. He'd ordered us each a cup of coffee, and mine was waiting for me as I slid into the booth across from him. "Let's order, and then we can compare notes," I suggested.

Aunt Ruthie came over just as I pulled off my jacket and set it aside. Tilly had settled herself under the table, so I slipped her the dog biscuit I had in my pocket. Coby ordered ham and eggs and I chose a waffle. I stirred some cream into my coffee and jumped right in.

"Before we begin, I want to ask you about the photo Armand Kowalski had in his vehicle."

Coby frowned. "I don't know him or where he got the photo. It must have been taken this past Sunday, while I was at the church where I was abandoned as a baby, asking the parishioners about the photo of the woman I believe to be my mother."

"When exactly did you arrive in Kalispell?" I asked.

"On Thursday of last week. I arrived early in the day, checked into my motel, and went to the church to speak to the pastor. As I mentioned, he's only been there about a decade, so he didn't know anything about a baby being abandoned so long ago. The pastor at that time had died, so I decided to show up on Sunday, hoping to find a longtime parishioner who remembered the woman in the photo. I didn't, but, as I said, I did find a woman who recognized the logo on the blanket. I stayed in Kalispell, following leads that went nowhere, and then, on Wednesday of this week, I headed to White Eagle."

"Had you done anything else with the photo between the time your adoptive father gave it to you and visiting Kalispell?"

Coby nodded. "The first thing I did was contact the agency who handled my adoption. The person I spoke to gave me what I thought was a canned response about confidentiality. I decided to go over his head, tracking down the email address of the head of the agency. I sent her a long email detailing what I knew and the unanswered questions that were haunting me and attached a copy of the photo my dad had given me, which I scanned in to my computer. A week later, she called me to say that while she was sorry she couldn't help me, my adoption records listed both my parents as *unknown*. I realized I wasn't going to get anywhere with the adoption agency, so I headed to Kalispell. It was the only lead I had, that

I'd been abandoned in a church there. The lead I got pointed me here."

"It's possible the man in the other car could have been following you ever since you contacted the adoption agency."

"Why would anyone be following me?" Coby asked. "It makes no sense. Besides, he was in front of me when the accident occurred."

"I didn't mean he was literally following you. I just meant he could have found out you were coming to White Eagle and decided to head in this direction as well. Are you sure you really have no idea who he could be?"

"I'm sure. I've never seen him before. Do you think he knew who I was and what I'm doing? Maybe he had an interest in the woman in the photo too."

I took a deep breath and let it out slowly. "I don't know. But the fact that a man who had a photo of you came to White Eagle on the exact same day you did makes me uncomfortable. I think we should tread carefully."

"I don't disagree, but I'm not going to stop looking for answers. Now that I have a lead on the identity of my biological mother, I can't seem to focus on anything other than finding her."

"I totally understand that."

We were quiet as our breakfast arrived. My mom walked away and I turned back to Coby. "So, you said you had a lead. What have you found?"

"I drove by the Honeycutt house yesterday and looked around," Coby began. "As would be expected of a place that's been vacant for five years, the yard is overgrown and there appears to be rot settling into the front porch. What I found most interesting, however, are the differences between what's in the photo and what exists there today."

"What do you mean?" I asked.

"First, I have this photo, but I don't have a date for it. I've been hoping the woman is my biological mother, and that I can use it to find her, but she could be just some other random person. When I saw the changes that had taken place on the property, I realized dating them could help me date the photo."

"I guess that makes sense. So what's different?"

Coby laid the photo on the table between us. "See this fence?" Coby pointed to a wrought-iron fence that ran along the front of the property. "Now there's a wooden picket fence in its place. I don't know when the wrought-iron fence was replaced, but the wooden one isn't new; the wood is worn, and the paint is chipped and faded. If we can find someone who remembers when the fence was replaced, we'll have a dot on the time line. If the fence was replaced more than thirty-five years ago, we'll know the woman in the photo isn't my mother because I'm only thirty-four. Or at least it isn't my mother when she was pregnant with me."

"Okay, I see what you're getting at. The changes can help you narrow in on a date for the photo. What else did you notice?"

Coby pointed to the photo again. "See this tree? It's a lot bigger now, and the initials *CW* are carved into the trunk right about here. If we can find out who carved the initials and when, we'll know the photo was taken before that."

Aunt Ruthie came by to refill our coffee, but I didn't miss a beat. "So we have the fence and the initials in the tree trunk, two time points. Anything else?"

"The only other thing I noticed was that the shutters on the front of the house are white now. In the photo they're black. I realize finding someone who remembers when the fence was replaced, shutters were painted, and a tree was carved after all these years will be difficult, but it seemed like something as opposed to the nothing I had before I visited the house."

I took a bite of my waffle, chewed, and swallowed. "We may not need to find someone who remembers. There are albums in the library with photos of the town and the surrounding area that go back more than a hundred years. I don't know for certain there are photos of the Honeycutt house, but I think it would be worth the time to look."

"I know you have to go to work, so if you want to tell me where the library is, I'll go there later."

I took out my phone. "I might be able to do you one better." I dialed the number Wilma had given me so we could arrange for our dogs to play. "Hey, Wilma, it's Tess. I have a friend in town doing some research who'd like to have a look at the town photo albums. I have to get to work, but if you don't mind coming in a few minutes early, I can bring him over and introduce him."

"I can be there by eight-thirty," Wilma replied. "I was going to go in early to catch up on shelving anyway."

"I need to start my route by nine so that would be perfect. We'll see you then." I hung up and looked at Coby. "Finish up. We have an appointment with Wilma at eight-thirty."

"Thanks so much. I'm so grateful for all your help."

"There's more. I have a meeting with Edith Honeycutt's neighbor, Dotty Norris, at noon. If you want to come with me, meet me at my Jeep at eleven forty-five."

"I'd love to come. Where will the Jeep be parked?"

"If today is another two-bag day, which I suspect it will be, I'll park in the center of town. I'll probably be pretty close to the diner, if you want to look on the street in this area."

"I'll be here."

After we finished breakfast I took Coby over to the library. I couldn't help but notice the look of interest on Wilma's face when I introduced them. I guess he was pretty good-looking and I estimated she was around my age, so I supposed the pair were well suited at least in terms of age. I explained to Wilma what Coby was looking for, then headed to the post office to pick up my deliveries for the day.

"Looks like another two-bagger," Queenie said as I checked in.

"Figured. I have a lot going on today, so I'll need to hurry. I have an appointment during lunch, so I'll be off route from around eleven forty-five until twelve forty-five. I'll have my cell if you need to get hold of me for any reason."

I picked up my bags and started toward my Jeep. I was going to need to drop and run at most of my stops or I'd never get through my route by five. The secret, I knew, was to avoid eye contact or even a cheery greeting if I could help it.

Miraculously, I managed to make 60 percent of my stops before I had to meet Coby. I headed to my Jeep, where he was waiting. I offered to drive, and he hopped into the passenger seat, greeting Tilly as we got underway.

"I'm very busy today, so my plan is to have a brief but hopefully informative conversation with Doris. She tends to go off on tangents, which we'll need to steer her away from at all costs."

"Got it. No tangents."

"Were you able to find anything in the library to help with dating the photo?" I asked as I pulled onto the highway that led out of town.

"Sort of. I was born in 1984. We found evidence that the fence was changed sometime between 1962 and 1989. That's a lot of years, but it's something. I didn't find a photo of the house with the white shutters it has now; the shutters were still black in a photo I found dated 1989. None of what I found proves the woman in the photo is my mother when she was pregnant with me, but nothing nullifies the theory either. Wilma's going to keep looking. She's very nice, and so helpful."

"She *is* a very nice woman. She's new to the area, so she won't have the background some of the old-timers do, but I'm sure she'll do what she can to help you find the answers you're looking for."

I pulled into Doris's drive and parked near the front door. I rolled down the window and told Tilly to stay. I could have dropped her off with Bree, but that hadn't occurred to me at the time I delivered her mail. Still, I didn't want to show up at the home of a woman I didn't know well with my dog in tow. It was a cool day and I parked in the shade. Tilly would be okay for a few minutes.

We got out of the Jeep and hurried up the walk to the front door.

"Tess, do come in," Doris greeted me after the first ring of the doorbell.

"This is Coby Walters," I introduced.

"And you're looking for your mother?" she asked as she showed us into the parlor.

"Yes, although I don't have a lot to go on."

Doris indicated we should sit on the sofa, and Coby handed her the photo.

"We hoped you might recognize the woman in this photo," I said.

Doris studied it. "She does look familiar." Doris tapped her chin with her index finger. "I think she stayed with Edith for a while, but I can't say I know much about her."

"Do you remember when she was in town?" I asked.

Doris shook her head. "It's been so long and my memory isn't what it used to be. It seems it must have been at least thirty years ago. Maybe more. If this is the girl I'm thinking of, she kept to herself most of the time, but Edith introduced her as her niece, Daisy. I only remember that because as far as I knew, Edith didn't have a niece, at least not one she'd ever mentioned. I suspected the girl was hiding from someone, but I didn't know that for certain."

"Do you remember ever hearing a last name?" I asked.

"No. I'm sure Edith never said. I wondered whether Daisy was the girl's real first name. She always seemed startled when anyone called her that."

"She looks to be very pregnant in the photo," Coby said. "Do you remember if she was still in the area after she had the baby?"

Doris slowly shook her head. "I'm not sure what happened to her. I asked Edith about her once, and all she said was that her niece had gone home. I don't know where home was, or even if that's where she really went. You might talk to Vern Sullivan."

"Vern Sullivan the feed store owner?" I asked.

"He worked for Edith as a handyman when he was in high school. I seem to remember him being around at about the same time Daisy was. He might know more about the girl and the reason for her visit."

I smiled at Doris. "Thank you. I'll stop by to speak to him. Before we go, we were wondering if you remembered when the shutters on the front of the Honeycutt house were painted from black to white."

"I guess it was a decade ago. Why do you ask?"

I explained our theory.

"I remember the girl being here at least thirty, maybe even forty years ago. The shutters were painted five years or so before Edith passed."

"And the fence? Do you remember when the fence was replaced?"

"After the great blizzard of 'eighty-six. Part of the old fence blew over and Edith decided to go with something a bit cheerier."

Okay, that helped. Coby was born in 'eighty-four and the fence was replaced two years later. We were beginning to narrow things down.

"Just one final question: Do you remember anyone named *CW* who might have carved their initials in the tree in front of the house?" I asked.

"Carl Willoughby. Carl was the son of Edith's maid, Penelope. He tagged along with his mother during the summer when he was off school."

"And when was that?" I asked.

Doris thought back. "I guess that would be during the eighties. Probably the mideighties. He works for the power company now."

I thanked Doris once again and then Coby and I returned to my Jeep.

"How are we supposed to find someone named Daisy when we don't have a last name?" Coby asked.

"We just keep asking around. That's the way these things work. You just keep whittling away at it until a picture begins to appear."

"Well, we know now that the woman in the photo could have been my mother when she was pregnant with me if the fence wasn't replaced until 'eighty-six and the tree and shutters came after that. Maybe this Vern Sullivan will know something."

"I'll call him as soon as we get back to town."

As it turned out, Vern wasn't at work that day and was out of town. He was willing to speak to us if we could come by his home the next day. I called Carl Willoughby, who was available to meet with us if we could come by his home after six. I was supposed to meet Bree then, but I supposed she could come with us to speak to Carl. Maybe the three of us could have dinner after. I hadn't had a chance to introduce Bree and Coby yet, but something told me they'd get along fine.

Chapter 6

I glanced at the clock on the wall as I hurried through the back door of the Book Boutique with minutes to spare. I'd decided to take Tilly home before meeting Coby and Bree, but once the kittens saw me, I knew I'd need to spend a few minutes playing with them before I fed them and left again. I'd told Coby to meet me at the Book Boutique at six, which meant I had five minutes to chat with Bree before he arrived.

"Thank you so much for being flexible," I said as I entered her office. "I know this was supposed to be our night and I really appreciate you letting Coby tag along."

"It's not a problem. After everything I've heard about him, I'm excited to meet him."

"Everything you've heard?"

"Wilma told me the guy is a total babe and so very nice, and your mom mentioned how well she thought the two of you were suited for each other."

"We're just friends, nothing more. You know how my mom likes to play matchmaker, but there's absolutely nothing between us other than the desire to solve his mystery."

"Megan from over at the Inn told me that Coby looks like a young Robert Redford."

I rolled my eyes. "Coby looks nothing like Robert Redford at any age."

"Maybe not, but I understand he's quite good-looking."

"I guess he is, but, as I said, I'm not interested, so if you see an opening, you're welcome to take it. Did you hear from your secret admirer today?"

Bree smiled. "I did." She set a book on her desk.

"He sent you a book? He does know you own a bookstore?"

Bree laughed. "I'm sure he does, but this is a first edition of one of my favorite books."

"So this guy knows you well enough to know what your favorite book is. How many guys would know that?"

"Not many," Bree admitted.

"You must have some idea who's sending you these gifts."

Bree shook her head. "I really don't. I've been wondering why anyone would go to so much trouble to retain his anonymity."

"Maybe the guy's just shy. Maybe he admires you but thinks he's unattractive and therefore not the type you typically date."

"Trust me, it doesn't matter in the least what the guy looks like. Whoever he is, he's made me smile. He's already a prince in my eyes."

I grinned. "I'm glad to hear that. I hope you aren't disappointed when the big reveal is made."

Bree frowned. "Are you sure you don't know who it is?"

I raised my hand in the air. "I swear, I have no idea, and if I did, I'd tell you."

"Okay. Just checking."

"I hear the back door. It must be Coby. Come on; I'll introduce you."

Once the introductions were made, the three of us climbed into Coby's rental and headed over to Carl's house.

"What beautiful sketches," I said, admiring the art on the wall as we walked into his house.

"Thank you. They're mine. I don't claim to be an artist, but I like to dabble."

"They're really good. I especially like this one of the geese on White Eagle Lake. It naturally elicits a feeling of calm and serenity."

"That's just what I was feeling when I drew it. So, how can I help you this evening?"

Coby showed Carl the photo and explained what we were after.

"Sure, I remember her," Carl said. "She was staying with Mrs. Honeycutt for a while. She was fun and beautiful, and I had a huge crush on her."

"Do you remember when that was?" Coby asked.

"It was the summer between seventh and eighth grade, so I guess it was 1983. Do you know her?"

"Maybe," Coby answered. "I understand she went by the name Daisy."

"That's right," Carl confirmed.

"Do you remember her last name?" Coby asked.

"I don't think she ever said. What I do remember is how nice she was. My mom was one of those overprotective sorts who made me go with her when she went to clean Mrs. Honeycutt's house even though I was old enough to stay home on my own. I think Daisy felt sorry for me, so whenever I was there she'd sit with me in the old swing on the porch and tell me stories about her past."

"What kind of stories?" Coby asked.

"Things that happened to her and things she saw, mostly. It seemed she'd been everywhere. She had stories about other states as well as cities like Paris, London, Berlin, even Cairo. I guess she must have been rich to travel so much."

"Did she ever mention who she traveled with?" Coby asked.

"Not that I recall. I think she was intentionally vague about the details. If you ask me, she was hiding from someone. Maybe her baby's father. She never, ever talked about the baby's father."

"Do you remember if she was still here when the baby arrived?" I asked.

Carl shook his head. "I was already back in school, so I wasn't around there as often, but I think she left town before the baby was born. I remember my mom having to go in on a weekend because Mrs. Honeycutt was throwing some sort of a party, and she needed her help with the heavy cleaning. Mom wasn't going to make me tag along, but I hadn't seen Daisy for quite a while, so I asked to go. Daisy was very pregnant, and I joked with her that the baby was going to show up before the following weekend, when Mom was going back to complete the party preparations. But by the next weekend Daisy was already gone. Mrs. Honeycutt gave me the gift she'd left for me and she said Daisy wanted me to know she'd enjoyed our friendship, but she had to go home."

"What kind of gift?" I asked. Although it really wasn't any of my business.

Carl got up, crossed the room, and took something out of a box on one of the bookshelves. He handed it to me.

"She left you this necklace?" I asked as I studied the silver medallion on a heavy chain.

Carl nodded. "She used to wear it, although she never said where she'd gotten it. I'd admired it on several occasions; I was really in to all things medieval back then, and I liked the dragon on it."

"Do you mind if I take a photo of it?" I asked.

Carl shook his head. "No, I don't mind. If you find her, will you let me know? I've always wondered what became of her and her baby."

We left Carl's and headed toward town to pick up my Jeep and then go out for dinner. As I suspected they would, Bree and Coby got along wonderfully. Coby was a reader, as was Bree, so a lot of the evening was spent discussing books the two had read and enjoyed. I'm not all that much of a reader myself, mostly because I never seem to find the time for books, so I mostly listened while I waited for the opportunity to cut out and head home. When I finally did make my excuses, Bree and Coby were deep in a discussion about modern genres and changing trends and they barely noticed when I left.

At home, I built a fire, then changed into my footie pajamas. I'd been so busy lately, I hadn't spent a lot of time with the kittens, so they were thrilled when it appeared I was in for the night. I clicked on the television and then settled onto the sofa with a quilt and a glass of wine. Within two minutes, all three animals had joined me.

The company was wonderful, but the show I was watching was tired and predictable, so I clicked it off and called Tony. If he was free, I might be able to talk him into some online gaming. It wasn't as much fun as playing in person, but it was a good option when neither of us wanted to make the trip between our homes.

"Hey, beautiful," Tony greeted me after a single ring. "To what do I owe the pleasure?"

"Bored," I admitted.

"I see. I thought you were going to dinner with Bree."

"I did, but Coby came along. They really hit it off, so it turns out it's just me and the kids tonight."

"I can come over if you want."

I sighed. I was certain I sounded more pathetic than I'd intended. "It's okay. You don't need to drive all the way over here just because there's nothing good on television. I hoped you might want to play online for a while."

"Actually, I'm already in town. I'll be there in ten minutes."

Well, that had worked out better than I'd hoped. Tony and I had been known to play video games well into the wee hours of the morning when I didn't have work the next day. Of course I did need to pick up the cookies for the shelter party before eight, so I supposed I shouldn't get to bed too late.

"Not that I'm not thrilled to see you, but why were you in town?" I asked when Tony and Titan arrived.

"I was meeting with Mike."

"My brother Mike?"

Tony took a seat on the sofa while Titan and Tilly walked around the room sniffing each other.

"He called me this morning and asked if I could help dig up information on Armand Kowalski."

"And what did you find?"

"Kowalski was born and raised in Poland. He came to the United States on a work visa in 1981. Most recently, he's worked for a company called Nowak Enterprises. It's based in San Francisco, but its parent company is in Slovakia."

"Okay, so why was this businessman from San Francisco who works for a Slovakian company following Coby?" I asked.

"I don't know. On the surface, there isn't a link between Coby and either Armand Kowalski or Nowak Enterprises. Mike called the company to inform them of the death of their employee. The woman he spoke to confirmed that Kowalski had worked for them for more than thirty years and was considered to be the right-hand man of his boss, Daniel Kovac, who's currently out of the country, meeting with *his* boss, Danko Milovich, a very wealthy man who owns companies all over the world."

I tucked my legs up under my body. "Does any of this make any sense to you?"

"No, I can't say that it does. The only take I have is that there's probably a whole lot more going on than meets the eye, and that always worries me."

"Yeah, it worries me as well."

Tony used the remote to turn on my gaming system. "How did your breakfast with Coby go?"

"Fine. He'd gone over to the Honeycutt place and noticed there'd been changes to the outside since the photo of the pregnant woman had been taken. He spent most of the day trying to date the changes."

"Did you find anything conclusive?"

"Not really. We still can't determine exactly when the photo was taken, but we're using the details to narrow things down a bit."

"Sounds like a technique I've used often."

"Like how we knew that first photo you found of my father was taken after he supposedly had died by looking at the buildings in the background?"

"Exactly." Tony handed me one of the controllers.

"Have you found anything else since we spoke yesterday?" I asked as Tony started the game and our quest began.

"Nothing significant, but I'm following up on a couple of things I'd rather not talk about until I have more data."

I returned my focus to the screen, screeching when Tony annihilated one of my ammunition warehouses. As much as I wanted to discuss the search for my father, at that moment I wanted to beat Tony at his own game even more.

Chapter 7

Saturday, February 10

"Oh good; I thought you'd forgotten to stop by," Hattie said as I hurried in through the front door of the bakeshop.

"I didn't forget; I'm just running late. Is this everything?" I nodded toward the piles of boxes on the counter.

"There's a cooler of punch in the back. If you'll grab that, I'll help you carry everything out."

I headed to the back room, where the cooler was waiting. I should have taken my own advice and kicked Tony out at a decent hour last night, but we were having so much fun and Titan and Tilly were so thrilled to be spending time together, before I knew it, the clock struck three and getting a good night's sleep was out of the question. Tony crashed on the sofa, so I had scrambled eggs and hot coffee waiting for me when I finally emerged from the bedroom in the morning.

"I hope this is enough for everyone," Hattie said as she helped me load the pink bakery boxes into the back of my Jeep.

"I'm sure it will be. Most folks who stop by are more interested in playing with the dogs than eating, although these cookies do look wonderful."

"Sugar cookies are my specialty. Do you have a lot of dogs to find placement for today?"

"I'm not sure. I know the shelter has been close to capacity, but all dogs that are brought in have to undergo a quarantine before they're eligible to be adopted, so the number being housed isn't necessarily the number available for adoption. I think we have quite a few to place."

"Well, good luck and have a good day."

I waved to her, jumped into the Jeep, and sped down the street toward the high school. The animal shelter was located next door to the only veterinary hospital in town, but Brady had wanted a larger place for the party and had convinced the high school to let him use their multipurpose room.

"I'm glad you're here," Brady said when I pulled up to the loading door.

"Sorry. I got a bit of a late start, but I have the punch and cookies, and Hattie even threw in cups and napkins. As soon as I get all this unloaded, I'll help with whatever else needs to be done."

"I was hoping you could take my van to pick up the last load of dogs. I brought eight and Lilly brought eight more, but there are five little guys still waiting for a ride."

"No problem. I'll pick them up as soon as I empty the Jeep. Do you need anything else while I'm out?"

"I think now that we have the punch and cookies we're in good shape."

Brady had done a wonderful job. The room was decorated with red, pink, and white streamers, and there were heart-shaped decorations taped to every wall. The long table for the cookies and punch was set off to the side, near the adoption application table, while most of the room was littered with bean bag chairs. The dogs that had already arrived seemed to be having a wonderful time playing with one another and the prospective adoptive parents hadn't even shown up yet.

By the time I returned to the party with the five smaller dogs, people were starting to arrive. I got them settled, grabbed a leash and a plastic bag, and started taking some of the dogs who had been there the longest out for bathroom breaks. Brady had designated a grassy area that had been cleared of snow and was well away from usual traffic lanes as bathroom central.

The event was well organized, and when two o'clock rolled around, all the dogs but one had been adopted. I picked up the small terrier mix and looked him in the eye. "Seems we still need to find a mom or dad for you, little one."

The dog growled at me with teeth bared.

"I think part of your problem might be your presentation. Most people don't want to adopt a pet who growls at them." The dog struggled to get down, so I set him on the ground. "Or a dog who doesn't like to be held or cuddled."

The little guy, whose name was Bruiser, was arguably a difficult placement because he was both ornerier than most of the dogs we placed as well as older. What he needed was a sweet older person who wouldn't feel the need to cuddle with the dog, who clearly preferred to be left alone.

"I'd say that was a success," Brady said after the last of the human guests had left with their new family members.

"We found homes for everyone but Bruiser."

Brady's smile faded. "He's a tough one, but I'm committed to keep trying until we find the perfect placement. Lilly and I need to stay to clean up. Do you mind dropping him back at the shelter?"

"I'd be happy to. I'll return Hattie's cooler as well."

Hattie closed early on Saturdays, so I drove around to the entrance off the alley. I'd opened the door to the cargo area to grab the cooler when Hattie came out to greet me.

"How'd it go?" she asked.

"Really well. We found homes for all but one of the dogs."

Hattie's smile faded. "Well, that's too bad. Which dog didn't get adopted?"

I pointed toward the dog crate in the back of the Jeep. "Bruiser. He's an older dog, which makes him harder to place, and he's a total grouch, which makes it doubly hard."

Hattie poked her head into the Jeep. "He's a cute little thing."

"He is. Until you touch him. Then he acts like he's going to take your head off."

"Bring him in and I'll give him a treat. I feel bad he didn't find a home."

I opened the door to the dog crate and attached a leash to Bruiser's collar, lifted him out of the Jeep, then followed him to the door from the alley into the bakeshop. Not only was it warm inside but it smelled delicious. Hattie knelt down with a dog cookie in her hand. Bruiser trotted over and very politely took it from her.

"I've been thinking about getting a pet now that Hap and I have split up and I live alone," Hattie mused.

"A pet is a great idea. I'd hate to go home to an empty house every night. We have several adult cats at the shelter if you want to come by to look."

"No." Hattie bent down and picked up Bruiser. "I don't think I'd enjoy a cat." I held my breath, anticipating bared teeth and deep growling, but Bruiser kissed Hattie on the cheek.

"Oh my God, he likes you," I blurted out with such surprise that I forgot to keep my voice down, which made Bruiser turn to me and show me his teeth.

"Of course." Hattie didn't seem fazed by Bruiser's show of irritation at my outburst. "I'm very likable."

I lowered my voice so I didn't anger the little dog again. "But Bruiser doesn't like anyone. He snaps at me, he snaps at Brady, he snaps at every potential adoptive parent."

Hattie scratched Bruiser under the chin. He wagged his tail and gave her another kiss before she set him down.

"Maybe Bruiser just has discriminating taste," Hattie said.

"I guess so. I don't suppose you'd like to take Bruiser home? For a trial, of course. There's no obligation if it doesn't work out."

Hattie looked down at Bruiser. "How about it? Do you want to come home with me?"

Bruiser barked once and then trotted to the door. There was no doubt about it, I had just witnessed a Valentine's Day miracle.

******

I left Hattie's and headed home. I found a note from Tony, saying he'd taken Tilly and the kittens home with him and would bring them back when I got home. I'd had the best time the night before and wouldn't mind a rematch. I'd promised Vern I'd stop by to talk to him, and I should check in with Bree and Coby too. I called Tony to say I had a few errands to run but if it was okay with him, I'd pick up a pizza and come to his place when I was done. He seemed delighted for the company and asked me to pick up some beer as well.

I called Coby and asked him if he wanted to go with me when I spoke to Vern, who'd been a handyman at the Honeycutt place while Daisy was staying there. He wanted to, so I arranged to pick him up at the Inn. When I got there, he thanked me for introducing him to Bree. Apparently, they'd had a wonderful time after I'd left the night before. Coby was just passing through, which was too bad; the two of them seemed perfect for each other.

Vern Sullivan owned the local feed store, so I'd arranged to meet him there. Saturday had the potential to be a busy day for him, so I hoped he had time to talk to us. I supposed we could come back later if he was busy, but I really wanted to help Coby wrap up his mystery as soon as possible.

As it turned out, Vern had been working in his office, not at the counter, so he did have time to speak to us. "Yeah, I remember her," he said after Coby showed him the photo. "Name was Daisy. Real cute little thing."

"I believe I might be related to her and am trying to track her down," Coby said. "I'd appreciate hearing anything you can tell me about her."

"Given the fact that you're about the right age, I'm going to go out on a limb and say you must be the baby she was carrying."

Coby looked at me. I raised a brow.

"I was adopted after being left at a church when I was an infant. This photo was left with me when I was dropped off. I don't know for certain that she's my mother; I'm trying to find out."

Vern ran a hand through his longish hair. "I'm not sure I know anything that will help you, but I'll tell you what I can."

"I'd be very grateful," Coby replied.

Vern cleared his throat, then began to speak. "I met Daisy on the day Edith brought her home. She had the look of a frightened deer about her, so I guessed immediately she was in some sort of trouble. I'm not sure how Edith knew her, but she had a kind heart and Daisy wasn't the first stray she'd brought home."

"I understand Edith told folks Daisy was her niece," I said.

"Yeah, that's what she told them, but I'm pretty sure it wasn't true. I'm not sure what the girl's real name was; I'm sure it wasn't Daisy. On the day she arrived, Edith told me Daisy would be staying with her for a while and I was to do what I could to make her comfortable. She also asked me to keep my eyes open and to let her know right away if I noticed any strangers lurking about. It didn't take a genius to realize the girl was running from someone and Edith was hiding her."

"Did either woman ever say anything to indicate who was after her?" I asked.

"No. Both were real careful not to say much of anything about who Daisy was, where she'd come from, or who she was hiding from. I always wondered what became of her. One day she was at the house and the next she was gone. I asked Edith, but all she would say was that she went home. Never did say where home was."

"We spoke to Carl Willoughby, who said Daisy disappeared just about the time she was due to give birth," I commented.

"Seems about right." Vern looked at Coby. "If you're the child she was carrying, I guess things didn't work out for her to keep her baby."

"Do you think she wanted to?" Coby asked.

"Oh, she wanted her baby all right. Something fierce. The poor little thing had this haunted look that took over completely when she spoke about her unborn child. She loved the baby, but I think she knew she couldn't keep him. It was tragic, really. To know that as soon as the baby was born your time together would come to an end."

I bit my lip to quell my tears. I felt so bad for the young woman and she wasn't tied to me in any way. I couldn't imagine how Coby felt.

"You know, if you really want to know what went on, you should try to get a look at Edith's attic," Vern suggested.

"Her attic?" I asked.

"Edith liked to keep mementos from her life. Not only did she collect things, she kept a journal she wrote in every day. I'm not sure who inherited the house, but I don't think anyone has been inside since she passed. I bet the answers you're looking for are boxed up and waiting for you to find them."

"That's a good idea. Thank you. I'll look in to it."

We chatted with Vern for a few more minutes and then headed to the car. When we were on the road, Coby asked if I had any idea how to locate Edith Honeycutt's next of kin to get permission to take a peek in the house.

"I have a friend who can find information like that. I'll ask him tonight and let you know tomorrow. This same friend has a facial recognition program as well, if you want him to run it against your photo. It's a long shot, but you never know."

"Do you trust this friend?"

"With my life."

"Okay, then let's do it. The more I find out about the woman in the photo, the more I hope she's my mother and I can find her."

"Yeah." I smiled at Coby. "Me too."

I dropped him off at the Inn, then drove into town to pick up beer and pizza to take to Tony's. I was looking forward to getting together with him tonight. Tony and I had been good friends since the seventh grade, but since he'd found the clues to my dad's past, our shared secret had brought us even closer than before. The more time I spent with the remarkable man, the more certain I was that I was very lucky to be his friend.

Chapter 8

Tony was outside gathering wood for the fire when I arrived. Titan and Tilly ran over to the Jeep as soon as I pulled into the drive. I grabbed the beer and pizza and followed Tony inside. Tang and Tinder, who'd been sleeping on Tony's sofa, trotted over to greet me when they realized I'd come in behind Tony.

"Looks like a storm is coming," Tony informed me after dropping his armload of wood onto the stack near the fireplace.

"I did notice the wind had picked up. I guess we could use some snow. It's been a light winter."

"The ski areas could certainly use a boost. I was up last week and the runs were getting pretty icy."

I set the pizza box on the counter, then went to the pantry for paper plates. I took a beer for myself and handed one to Tony, then put the rest in the refrigerator.

"Before we get involved in the game and I forget to ask, I need you to do me a couple of favors related to the mystery I'm trying to help Coby solve," I said.

"The missing mother?" Tony clarified.

"Exactly."

Tony picked up a large slice of pizza and slipped it onto his plate. He licked his fingers, then grabbed a napkin and his beer and headed to the sofa. "What do you need me to do?"

I grabbed my own beer and pizza and sat down beside him. "First, I have Coby's permission for you to run the facial recognition program on the photo of the woman he believes to be his mother. I warned him it was a long shot, but I suppose it makes sense to take any shot we're offered."

"I'll set up the program after dinner. Anything else?"

"We want to look inside the Honeycutt place. We'll need permission from the current owner. I was hoping you could find out who that might be."

"I can do that, although anyone can pull information related to property ownership. It's a matter of public record. Do you know if anyone has lived in the house since the woman who owned it died?"

"No one has lived there; as far as I can tell, no one has even visited. The house and the surrounding land has got to be worth a significant amount of money. I'm kind of surprised whoever inherited it hasn't put it on the market. I suppose there could be some sort of a dispute between family members tying the place up." I got up, walked to the table, grabbed a second slice of pizza, and slipped it onto my plate. "By the way, thanks for bringing the kids over here today. I feel bad the kittens are left alone so much. I'm sure they enjoyed hanging out here with you."

"No problem. I enjoyed having them," Tony answered as I sat back down next to him. "And I know Titan has enjoyed spending time with Tilly. Did you work it out to hang out over here tomorrow?"

I nodded. "I told my mom I had plans. She actually seemed fine with the whole thing, so she may have plans of her own." I jumped as a gust of wind pounded into the side of the house. "With the storm coming, I should have made plans to stay over in one of your guest rooms."

"I have an extra toothbrush and a T-shirt you can sleep in. The storm is supposed to roll in at around eight with heavy snow overnight. It would be best if you stayed."

I glanced out the window at the dark sky. "Thanks. I might just do that."

"Let's take care of the facial recognition and home ownership information you want before we start to play. I have a new game to preview that looks pretty awesome. I have a feeling once we get started, we won't want to be interrupted."

Tony put the leftover pizza in the refrigerator and then I followed him down to his computer room. I wasn't sure how much he'd invested in computers, monitors, and other electronics, but I thought the room must hold a million dollars' worth of equipment. Tony logged onto the system from one of the many stations he had set up. It only took him a few minutes to find out that when Edith passed away, her entire estate had been left to the son of one of her cousins, who lived in Chicago.

"I have a phone number if you want to call him," Tony offered.

"Thanks. I do want to talk to him."

I made my call while Tony logged onto a different computer he used to run the facial recognition software. The man who owned the Honeycutt house was fine with Coby and me going inside once I explained what we were looking for. An attorney in Kalispell had the key, and he'd get in touch with him about giving it to me.

I hung up and crossed the room to find Tony staring at the computer screen with a frown on his face.

"Is there a problem?" I asked.

"Not a problem. Just something curious."

"Curious how?" I stood directly behind him, peering over his shoulder. On the screen was the image of a man standing on a bridge overlooking a wide body of water. The photo had been cropped tightly so the scenery behind the bridge was obscured, making it difficult to discern exactly where the bridge was located. "What am I looking at?"

"This was pinged by my software as a possible match for your father."

"It doesn't look like him," I said.

"At first glance I would agree, but the longer I look at the photo, the less certain I am that this isn't your father as a much younger man." Tony pointed to the screen. "The program looks for spatial similarities such as the distance between eyes, facial length and width, height of forehead, etc. The man in this photo has a beard and mustache, but the overall shape of the face is very similar. And look at the eyes." Tony pointed to the eyes, then held up one of the other photos he'd found next to it.

"I guess it could be him. He looks so different, but now that I think about it, I see what you mean. Do you know when or where the photo was taken?"

"No, but based on the lack of wrinkling around the eyes, I'm going to say this man is significantly younger than the one in the other two photos I found."

I continued to stare at the photo on the screen. "I'm still not sure it's him, but I suppose it could be. Can we figure out where the photo was taken?"

"Maybe." Tony typed in some commands and then sat back. "It'll take a few minutes. Did you get hold of the man who inherited the Honeycutt house?"

"Yes, and he's fine with my looking inside. An attorney in Kalispell has a key. I'm sure his office will be closed tomorrow, but I'm hoping he'll allow me to pick it up anyway."

"If we can get in touch with him, I'll go there with you tomorrow."

Tony's computer dinged. He typed in a few commands and looked at the screen. "The photo was taken in Norway."

"Norway? I don't remember my dad ever saying he'd been there. In fact, I'm sure I remember him saying on several occasions that although he'd been back and forth across this country many times as a long-haul trucker, he'd never been anywhere fun or interesting and hoped to get to Europe one day."

"Hang on. I want to try something." Tony typed in another set of commands. After several minutes, an image of a young man with features similar to my father appeared.

"That looks like the man on the bridge."

"I think it is. The program indicated a ninety-five percent chance of a match between the man on the bridge and the one in this photo."

"Who are we looking at?"

"This is the passport photo of a man named Jared Collins, dated 1981."

"Jared Collins? Are you sure?"

Tony nodded.

I stared at the photo but still wasn't sure. On one hand, the man in the photo did have features very similar to the ones I remembered my dad having. The eyes especially were the exact same color and shape. Jared Collins's passport photo would have been taken before my father and mother were married. If my father and Jared Collins were the same person, he must have changed his name before meeting my mother.

"Do you think you can find additional photos of Jared Collins? Maybe photos from differing perspectives will give us a better idea of whether Jared Collins and Grant Thomas are the same person."

"I'll keep looking. It would help if we could find a photo of Jared Collins without a beard. I'll also look for photos of Grant Thomas taken before 1981. He must have had a driver's license, and probably took school photos as well."

"I wonder if my mom has photos of my dad as a boy and young man."

"I suppose it would be worth it to ask her. Find out what high school he went to. We should be able to pull up a yearbook online."

"Yeah, okay. I'll look for an opportunity to ask her."

The storm had arrived with full force by the time Tony and I made our way from the computer room up to the living area of the house. We enjoyed a very closely matched game of Alien Wars before deciding to turn in for the night. I'd only been sleeping for a few hours when a loud crash outside my bedroom window woke me. Wrapping a blanket around my T-shirt-clad body, I made my way out to the living room, where I found Tony tossing another log on the fire.

"Power's out," he informed me. "I have a generator if we need it."

I sat down on the sofa, keeping the blanket wrapped tightly around my body. "It's nice sitting here by the fire. I don't think we need lights. Did you hear that crash?"

"I think a tree branch may have fallen onto my shed. I bet I'll have damage to deal with when the storm passes. Where are the kittens?"

Tilly had jumped up onto the sofa and laid her head in my lap. "Still curled up under the covers in the guest room. They'll probably come out when they figure out I'm not coming back right away." I flinched as the wind created another loud crash. "I hope your shed isn't completely destroyed by the time the storm is over." I glanced out the window. All I could see was a sheet of white as the blizzard raged.

"I'll deal with the damage later."

"It feels like the house is going to blow over when the gusts hit it," I commented.

"I wouldn't worry about it. The house is sturdy, and we have lots of wood to keep it warm."

Tony sat down next to me. I put my head on his shoulder. It was kind of nice to curl up by the fire while snow blanketed the house.

"Do you think it was all a lie?" I asked after several minutes of silence.

"What do you mean?" Tony put his arm around my shoulders, cradling my body against his.

"I've been thinking about my dad. I guess up to now, I've been operating under the assumption that even though my dad lied about his death and has been living another life since, whatever happened to cause him to leave occurred at the time of his disappearance. I believed it was that occurrence that changed the trajectory of his life. But with this new information—that he might have had another name and traveled to Norway even before marrying my mother—has me wondering if his whole life was a lie. Was he ever the man I thought he was?"

"I wish I had the answers you need."

I stared into the flames in the fireplace. "I remember when I was four or five. My dad decided he wanted to spend more time at home, so he found a job doing a day run that allowed him to return to the family every night. He didn't make as much money, so he went back to long-haul trucking after only a couple of years, but during those years he was home, I can remember him not only joking around with my brother during dinner but reading me stories when he put me to bed. It was the best time of my childhood."

"Just because the man you knew as Grant Thomas may have been living another life doesn't mean he didn't love you."

I snuggled into Tony's warmth. "I know. At least I think I know. Dad was gone a lot when I was growing up, but there were a lot of awesome times as well. I remember him as a man who worked hard to take care of his family, and although he was away a lot, he was really *there* for us when he was home. Looking back, I have to wonder if my mom suspected there was more to Dad's absences than met the eye."

"You don't know for certain your dad wasn't doing exactly what he said he was doing," Tony reminded me. "All we really know is that unless he has a double who looks exactly like him, he didn't die fourteen years ago, and he may have been in Norway before marrying your mom and starting a family. Keep in mind, a lot of people visit Norway. It's a beautiful country and a popular vacation spot."

"Maybe, but not everyone has a second identity." I yawned as I let the warmth of the fire combined with the warmth of Tony's body lull me toward sleep. "If the man on the bridge is my father, I don't understand why he specifically said he hadn't been to Europe. Why would he lie about something like that? It's not like anyone would care whether he'd visited Europe as a young man. It seems like such a ridiculous thing to keep secret."

"Grant Thomas didn't visit Europe. At least not as far as we know. *Jared Collins* visited Europe. If Jared Collins and Grant Thomas are the same man, chances are the former had something to hide. Perhaps it had something to do with his time in Europe, so he lied about having ever been there."

"Maybe. I hate the idea that my dad may have been someone other than who he said he was, living some sort of a secret life."

Tony tightened his hand around mine. "I know. And I'm sorry."

"Don't you think it's odd that you looked for evidence Dad hadn't died in the accident we were told about for more than a decade before you found the first photo a couple of months ago, and then have found two more photos in the past week?"

Tony leaned his head against mine. "It's not really all that surprising. For one thing, the software I'm using now is much more advanced than anything I had before. And the more photos we find, the more information the program has to use as a guideline. I imagine new photos of your father will start coming in at much closer intervals." Tony paused, then added, "I do have to ask again, though, if you're sure you want me to keep looking. You have fond memories of your dad. Maybe you should hang on to those and move on with your life."

I yawned. "I can't move on. I have to know."

Chapter 9

Sunday, February 11

I must have fallen asleep because the next thing I knew, I was lying on the sofa with Tilly and both kittens tucked in close to me. I slowly sat up and glanced out the window. It was still overcast, but the snow had stopped. I pulled the blanket more closely around my shoulders, taking a minute to fully wake. I didn't see or hear Tony, but I could hear the snowblower in the drive. I unfolded my body and stood up. The fire had warmed the room, but the floor was still cold, so I went to the room I'd briefly used and grabbed the clothes I'd worn the day before. After dressing and brushing my teeth, I headed into the kitchen, where a pot of coffee waited. Apparently, the power had come back on during the night.

I looked out the window and saw Tony was almost done with the drive, so I opened the refrigerator, checking for something to make for breakfast. Deciding on scrambled eggs and bacon, I started our meal before looking for phone messages. There was one from the attorney who had the key to the Honeycutt house, letting me know I could pick it up anytime it was convenient. He'd left his phone number so I could make arrangements. I also had a text from Bree, saying she and Coby had gone to dinner the previous evening and stumbled on a clue to the whereabouts of the woman who'd made the blanket Daisy was holding in the photo. I texted Bree back to tell her I was making breakfast but would call her in a little while.

By the time the bacon was done, I could hear Tony stomping the snow off his boots. I poured the eggs in a pan just as he wandered in from the mudroom in his stocking feet.

"Something smells good," he said.

"Bacon. I figured I'd make breakfast while you did the drive. It looks like we got at least a couple of feet."

"I'd estimate three. The driveway is clear, but we'll need to wait for the plow to come by to do the road." Tony crossed the room and poured himself a cup of coffee. "Did you hear back from the man with the key?"

"I did. He left a number. I'll call him after breakfast." I mentioned Bree's text as well. "I know we planned to just chill today, but if the road is plowed in time, would you mind driving me into Kalispell to pick up the key? I'd love to get a look at the attic in case Edith kept the journals Vern told me about."

Tony shrugged. "Whatever you want to do is fine with me."

As it turned out, the plow came by while we were eating. I called the attorney, who was okay with meeting us at his office at noon. I took the dogs out for a quick walk while Tony showered and dressed, and then we drove to my cabin so I could clean up as well. We'd left the animals at Tony's because I'd have to come back to pick up my Jeep anyway. We headed back to White Eagle with the key in hand and the Honeycutt place, where Coby and Bree were meeting us.

"It feels sort of weird to be walking around in the home of a woman who's no longer with us," I said after we entered through the front door.

"Had you ever been here when Edith Honeycutt was alive?" Coby asked.

"No, never. I always imagined it would be beautiful inside." I looked around at the artwork on the walls and the antique furniture that was covered with dust but still quite amazing. "I wonder why the new owner hasn't done anything with the place. The art alone must be worth a fortune."

"He might not need the money and just hasn't taken the time to deal with his inheritance," Bree offered.

I glanced at the open stairway. "It sounded like the keepsakes and journals would be stored in the attic. Let's head up."

Tony took my hand and led me up the stairs, Coby and Bree following behind. The attic was at the top of another stairway from the second story of the house. It occurred to me that the door to the attic could be locked, but Tony turned the handle and it opened easily. There was a window inside, but the shutters over it were closed, blocking out the light. I found a switch on the wall for the overhead light, but the electricity had been turned off. I used the flashlight on my phone to make my way around the room while I opened the shutters to let some light in.

"There's a lot of stuff in here," Bree said.

"It'll be hard to find what we're looking for, especially because we aren't sure where it might have been stored," I agreed.

"Maybe we should just start opening boxes," Coby suggested. "I'd think any box that contains photos or books could be helpful."

I walked to the back of the room, where there were boxes stacked almost to the ceiling. Bree followed. I stood on tiptoe to take down the first box. I set it on the floor and opened the lid. "Looks like dishes."

"This one has dishes as well," Bree said from her position next to me.

I opened the next box in the pile to find old linens. "While we're looking, tell me about the clue you brought up in your text."

"Coby and I ran into Sue Wade last night," Bree said, mentioning the owner of Sue's Sewing Nook. "She said Gilda Swan, who owned The Cat's Meow, moved to Missoula. I guess they stayed in touch because Sue had Gilda's phone number. I called Gilda this morning and asked about the blanket Daisy was holding in the photo. She said she gave it to her as a gift."

I set the box I'd been going through to my left and took the next one from the pile. "Did she know anything more about her?"

"Gilda said Daisy wore a bracelet she recognized as being associated with a private school her cousin attended in Boston. She asked her about it, and Daisy said she hadn't gone there, but she grew up in Boston and the bracelet was a gift from a friend who went there. I know that isn't a lot to go on, but it's something."

"It could help us narrow our search."

I looked across the room to where Tony and Coby were looking through boxes in the front of the attic. "Any luck?" I asked.

"Not so far," Coby said, setting the box he was looking though aside. "It's going to take hours to go through all this."

"Oh, hey," Bree screeched from behind me. "I think I found something."

I turned around to look at the box, which held small leather journals, each neatly labeled and dated. "Look for one dated 1984 or thereabouts," I said.

Bree picked up the first journal, opened it, looked at the first page, then set it aside. She continued to do so until she had worked her way through half the box. "I found 1982 and 1985, but no '83 or '84."

"Keep looking," I urged. "Maybe they're out of order."

By the time Bree had gone through the entire box she'd determined 1983 and 1984 weren't with the others.

"Maybe if Daisy was running from someone, Edith hid or disposed of the journals to ensure they didn't fall into the wrong hands," I suggested.

"It'd think she'd only do that if she had reason to believe someone would come looking for them," Coby said.

Tony stood in the center of the room and slowly looked around. His eyes settled on a trunk in the corner of the room. He headed in that direction only to find it was locked. After a few minutes of going through nearby boxes, he found a small carpenter's file, which he used to open the trunk. Inside were items of value: jewelry, household items made of silver, and the journals from 1983 and 1984.

Tony handed the journals to Coby, who opened the first one and began to thumb through it. After a moment he began to read aloud. "'I knew the moment I saw the girl on the ferry that she needed my help. Not only did she appear to be traveling alone, but the cautious look in her eyes as she studied everyone aboard led me to believe she had grown accustomed to watching her back.'"

"What ferry?" I asked.

Coby looked back down at the book. "It doesn't say. There aren't any ferries around here, so I guess we'll have to assume Edith met Daisy while she was traveling."

"That makes sense. What else does it say?"

Coby looked back down at the journal. He flipped through the next few pages and then said, "A few days later, Edith writes that the girl has agreed to stay with her until her baby is born but has refused to reveal her name. Edith indicates it doesn't matter to her, and she decides to refer to her as Daisy."

"I assumed Edith knew Daisy's real identity, but it sounds like she didn't," I said.

"That is the way it sounds," Coby agreed. "Edith doesn't say a lot about the girl at all. Most of the passages that follow have to do with the hot weather, her garden, and her plans to travel to Europe the following winter. She does mention that Daisy seems to be retreating into herself more and more each day as the birth of her child nears. She's worried about her and wonders who Daisy might be running from and how she can help."

"Maybe we should bring the journals with us," I said. "We can read thorough them carefully, then return them when we're done."

The others agreed that taking our time with the journals was a good idea. The only other thing I found of any interest was a sketchbook with pencil drawings. There were a lot from different settings, but at least some of them appeared to have been of the house. I had no reason to believe Daisy had even been staying in White Eagle when the drawings were made, but my instinct told me to take a closer look at the sketchbook, so I took it with us as well.

We left the house and stopped at a nearby pub for a beer and orders of chicken wings and nachos. It was Sunday afternoon, so it was crowded, but we managed to find a table near the fireplace. There was a ski competition on the television over the bar, which reminded me that I needed to find some time to head up to the slopes, especially now that we had all this fresh snow. Coby had brought the journal in with him and was reading to us while we waited for our food.

"Here's a passage where Edith refers to the baby's father," Coby said. "'Daisy seems to be terrified of the father of her child. It makes me wonder who he is and how they came to be a couple. Daisy isn't going to keep her child. I suspect that's to cut all ties between the baby and his father.'" Coby set the journal aside when the wings and nachos were delivered.

"If Edith is correct, and Daisy planned to hide any link between her baby and herself, I wonder why she left the photo," Bree mused.

I picked up a wing but paused before taking a bite. "That's a really good question. Hiding her baby from someone who'd potentially come looking for him seems to explain why she left the baby at a church anonymously and didn't pursue traditional adoption. She didn't want there to be a trail leading back to her. But the inclusion of the photo does seem counterintuitive if that was her goal."

"What if my mother wasn't the one who left me at the church?" Coby asked. "What if she left me with Edith, who promised to make sure I ended up with a good family?"

"And it was Edith who left the photo as some sort of link back to White Eagle," I finished.

"Do you think my mother is still alive?"

No one answered, probably because none of us had any idea. Daisy was a young woman when Coby was born, so agewise, she could easily still be alive, but if she'd been involved with bad people, they could very well have wanted her dead.

After a bit, I asked Bree about her secret admirer. We were in a noisy bar, after all, and talk of the possible violent death of Coby's mother seemed incongruent with the mood of the room.

"I received a necklace yesterday. All the gifts have been delivered to the store, and it's closed today and tomorrow. Valentine's Day is on Wednesday, so I imagine that may be it."

"And you still have no idea who sent the gifts?" I asked.

"I don't, and trust me, I've spent an inordinate amount of time trying to figure it out. If you think about it, the field of possible suspects is limited because the gift giver seems to know me well. Not only was the book one of my favorites but the necklace has my birthstone."

"Maybe it's an ex who's looking for a second chance," Coby suggested.

Bree frowned. "It could be an ex, but most of the men I've been involved with weren't thoughtful enough to send me gifts when we were dating."

"It's not all that hard to find someone's birthday or their favorite book," Tony commented. "That information is probably all over your social media accounts."

Bree leaned back and looked at Tony. "That's true. The gift giver could be someone I've never even met."

"Okay, how did an incredibly sweet gesture suddenly turn into something creepy?" I asked.

"I'm not saying it's creepy," Tony countered. "I do think Bree should be careful, though. If the gift giver suggests you meet in person at any point, I'd be very cautious about agreeing unless you find out exactly who you're dealing with."

After we finished eating, Bree and Coby left together and Tony and I went back to his house. I had work tomorrow, so I needed to keep my eye on the clock and get home at a decent hour. I probably should have taken the Jeep with me when we went back to my cabin earlier, but I was focused on the mystery and didn't think about all the extra trips I'd be taking between Tony's home and mine.

When we arrived at Tony's there was a black Suburban with tinted windows in the driveway.

"It looks like you have company."

Tony frowned. "It does seem to be the case."

Tony pulled up to his regular parking space and turned off the engine. "Wait here."

I wanted to argue, but the look on his face left no room for argument. I cracked the window so I could hear what was going on.

"Are you Antonio Marconi?" the driver of the vehicle, who had gotten out of the Suburban and was wearing a black suit with a white shirt, asked.

"That depends. Who are you?"

Another man wearing an identical black suit emerged from the SUV. Suddenly, I had the sensation of being an extra in a mobster movie.

"I understand you've been looking for this woman." The man who had been seated in the back of the Suburban said as he handed Tony a photo. "Have you found her?"

"Who are you exactly?" Tony asked.

"I'm a representative of Danko Milovich, Maria's husband. I'm going to ask you again: have you found her?"

"No, I haven't. Until this moment, I didn't even know her name was Maria." Tony paused, then looked the man in the eye. "If you're a representative of this woman's husband, shouldn't you know where she is?"

"It would seem." I gasped as the man reached into his pocket. I thought he'd been going for a gun, but all he came back with was a business card. "This is my number. I want you to call me immediately if you locate Maria. It's imperative I speak to her before anyone else does."

I didn't hear Tony's reply if he offered one. It looked as if he just watched the man as he got back in the SUV, and the vehicle drove away. I got out of the truck and joined Tony. "Who was that?"

"He claims to be a representative of Danko Milovich, Maria's husband."

"And who's Maria?"

"It seems that's Daisy's real name." Tony looked at the card in his hand.

I frowned. "Why does the name Danko Milovich sound so familiar?"

"He's the man I told you about, who owns businesses all over the world, including Nowak Enterprises, the company Armand Kowalski worked for."

"So the man Daisy was married to, the man who's most likely Coby's birth father, and the man Daisy was running from is the same one who owns the company the man who was in the accident with Coby worked for."

"Exactly."

I felt chills run down my spine. "I think this just got a whole lot more complicated."

Chapter 10

Monday, February 12

I decided to begin my route that morning at Grandma Hattie's Bakeshop. I wanted to see how she was doing with Bruiser. She'd taken him for a trial adoption on impulse, and I knew he could be a difficult dog for any owner, especially one who didn't have a lot of experience. When I arrived at the bakeshop, Bruiser was laying quietly on a heated dog bed behind the counter. He glanced up at me when I approached but quickly lowered his head and went back to sleep.

"It looks like Bruiser has settled in just fine." I set a pile of mail on the counter. Tilly sat down next to my feet and waited patiently for Hattie to give her a treat, as she always did.

"Bruiser and I are getting along just fine with one exception."

I glanced at the dog, who seemed to be more relaxed than I'd ever seen him. "Oh, and what's that?"

"He hates Hap."

I couldn't help but frown. "Really? More so than anyone else?"

"Apparently. I took Bruiser home on Saturday evening and everything was going great. Then Hap came over on Sunday for our regular weekly dinner, and Bruiser immediately started barking and growling at him. Hap offered Bruiser his hand to show he wasn't a threat and Bruiser snapped at him. I ended up closing Bruiser in my bedroom so Hap and I could enjoy our meal. I'd pretty much decided the arrangement wasn't going to work out after all, but then Hap left and my next-door neighbor stopped by, and Bruiser was a complete angel."

"Did Hap hug you when he came over?" I asked.

"Well, yes. That's his usual way of greeting me."

"Did the neighbor hug you?"

"No. She just came in and sat down at the kitchen table."

"Have people been coming and going all morning?" I asked. Hattie had already been open for more than two hours and she tended to get a lot of business first thing.

"Yes. It's been a busy morning. Why?"

I glanced behind the counter. "Has Bruiser been laying there all morning?"

"Yes, and he hasn't made a peep. He really has been the prefect angel."

I motioned for Tilly to stay, then I walked around to the side of the counter where the opening to the area behind the counter was. "Walk over to me and give me a hug," I instructed.

Hattie did as I'd asked, and Bruiser immediately jumped up and started growling and barking. Tilly popped up, I was sure to come to my rescue, so I took a step back and Hattie returned to her place behind the counter. Bruiser sat firmly on Hattie's foot, as if daring me to try to approach her again.

"Bruiser is just protecting you. When Hap hugged you, he interpreted his movement as being aggressive. My advice is to have Hap over again, but this time tell him not to hug you or even touch you when Bruiser is in the room. Chances are, once Bruiser gets used to Hap, he'll allow him to approach you. I have to warn you, it could take a while if he's already decided Hap is the enemy."

Hattie leaned over and picked up Bruiser, who looked at me with distrust but seemed content to be in Hattie's arms. "Okay, I'll try that," Hattie replied. "I really have grown fond of the little guy. I'd hate it if he couldn't learn to like Hap."

I left Hattie's and continued down the street. Most of the merchants were too busy to chat, so I was making good time today. The bookshop was closed, as it was every Sunday and Monday between New Year's and the first of June, so I didn't have to worry about Bree slowing me down. Tony had promised to do some digging into Danko Milovich, and I was anxious to hear what he'd found. If Daisy really was his wife, I wondered why she'd run away and how long she'd been missing. I sort of doubted this Milovich fellow had been looking for his wife for thirty-five years, which led me to believe she'd gone back to him after she'd had her child, and then for some reason had run away again.

Of course, for all we knew, Daisy could have given birth to Coby before she even met Milovich. If that was the case, she would have been running away from a different man back then, and was running from Milovich now. At least I assumed she was running; the man hadn't said as much. What he'd said was that Maria's husband didn't know where she was. Maybe Maria was the type to run when things got tough. For all I knew, she could have run away from dozens of men in her lifetime.

When I arrived at Sisters' Diner with the mail, the first thing I noticed was the smile on Mom's face and the twinkle in her eye. She was busy, so she did little more than wave before scurrying off to take an order, but even her movement across the restaurant seemed to have a bounce to it.

"Mom's in a good mood today," I said to Aunt Ruthie after Tilly and I entered the kitchen to say hi.

"Romero Montenegro is in town."

"In town?" I asked, surprise evident in my voice.

"He showed up on Saturday and plans to stay through next weekend. Your mom is over-the-top happy. Happier than I've seen her since she first met your father."

When I'd found out Mom had a pen pal halfway across the world, I wasn't concerned, but now that he was here, I realized I needed to find out more about the guy. "He isn't staying with her, is he?"

"No. He has a room at the Inn. At least for now."

At least for now? What did that mean?

"How well do you know this man?" I asked Ruthie.

"Not well at all. He stopped in last summer on his way through town. It was slow that day, so your mom had time on her hands and stopped by his table and struck up a conversation. She recommended some must-see sights along the route he was taking and he seemed grateful for the insights. When he returned home to Italy, he sent your mom a thank-you card and they continued to correspond. I think she was as surprised as anyone when he showed up this weekend, but she was also very happy to see him."

"Am I a horrible person to be uncomfortable with the whole thing?"

Ruthie shook her head. "It's understandable you would feel protective toward your mother. I'm not sure I want to be around when Mike finds out she's entertaining a stranger from another country."

Ruthie had a point. Mike was even more protective of our mother than I was. When Dad died, he'd taken over as head of the house, a role he took and continues to take very seriously.

"Do you think we can trust this man?" I asked.

Ruthie shrugged. "I don't know him. I think I've said maybe five words to him in total. But your mom seems to trust that he's exactly as he seems to be, and I have no reason to doubt her judgment."

Ruthie had a point, but it was beginning to look like Mom had married a man who'd fooled us all for almost twenty years. If she could be duped once, she could be duped again.

Mom was still busy when I returned to the dining area, so I waved to her and went on my route. I'd spoken to her on the phone briefly on Saturday and she hadn't said a thing about her Italian boy toy being in town then. I wasn't sure if I should be irritated or worried about the situation.

By the time I'd returned to my Jeep to trade out my empty mailbag for the second full one, I'd managed to work myself up quite a lot. I'd made good time that morning, so I took a minute to call Tony. If Mr. Montenegro was going to woo my mother, I was going to find out everything there was to know about him.

"Hey, Tony," I greeted him when he answered my call. "I need you to do me another favor."

"Is this regarding Daisy, or Maria, or whatever her real name is?"

"Actually, no. I need you to do a background check on Romero Montenegro. He lives in Italy and is currently visiting White Eagle."

"Okay. Can I ask why??"

"He's dating my mother."

"And this upsets you?"

"I won't go so far as to say it upsets me; it makes me uncomfortable. Other than his name, I don't know a thing about him."

Tony paused, then said, "Okay; I'll see what I can find. I found some stuff about Maria Milovich, by the way. Do you want to come over here after work so we can go through everything?"

"That sounds like a good plan. I'll bring us some dinner."

I hung up the phone and continued with my route. It was a cold day with flurries in the air, but it didn't appear we were in for any serious snow at least for the rest of the week. I loved living where there were four seasons and I enjoyed the snow most of the time, but I had to admit that by this point in the winter I was daydreaming about the longer, warmer days of summer. I managed to make really good time and was finished with my route by four-thirty. I tossed the empty bags into the back of the Jeep and headed to the post office to drop them off so they could be packed with the mail I'd deliver the next day. When I arrived, Queenie informed me there was a card for Mike that hadn't made it in with the day's mail. She wondered if I wanted to drop it off at his office then or if she should just put it in with tomorrow's mail. I told her I'd take it and went in that direction.

"Afternoon, Frank," I greeted Mike's partner as I entered the local branch of the sheriff's office. "I have a card for Mike. Is he in his office?"

"Last I checked, he was on the phone."

I headed down the hallway to find he was still on the phone. I waited in the hallway while he finished his order for twelve heart-shaped cookies with red frosting and white sprinkles before knocking on the door to let him know I was there. "I have a card for you." I held it up in the air.

"Just toss it on the desk. Is Tilly with you?"

"She's out front chatting with Frank. Aren't you going to open your card?"

"I will later."

Part of me wanted to tell Mike about Romero Montenegro, but another didn't want to light any fires I couldn't put out. I thought I'd wait to see what Tony had to say about the man before I said anything to Mike. Of course, it was possible someone else would say something to him before I had a chance to do it, but in the spirit of harmony between family members, that was a risk I was willing to take.

I chatted with Mike for a few more minutes before going on my way back to the post office. By the time the mailbags were turned in and I'd chatted with Queenie, it was almost five. I decided to go home, change my clothes, pick up the kittens, and then go back into town to pick up Chinese food before driving up the mountain to Tony's house. Everything would have worked out just as I planned if I hadn't seen something on the side of the road after I'd turned off Main Street and onto the highway leading out to my cabin. I pulled over and got out to check it out.

"Oh no, what happened to you?" I asked the medium-size black-and-white dog who appeared to have a broken leg. "Were you hit by a car?"

The dog whined as I slowly approached, bent down, and reached out a hand to him. "I'm not going to hurt you," I said as gently as possible. "I need to take you to see Doc Baker, so I'm going to have to lift you. Is that okay?"

The dog looked spooked, and I was afraid he'd either bite me or even jump up despite his injury and try to get away.

"I'm just going to put my hand on your head," I said slowly, moving my hand in the dog's direction. He began to growl, but he was also wagging his tail, and I wasn't sure what he would do next. Once my hand was on his head, I slowly worked it down his body, still speaking softly to him. After a minute he stopped growling.

"Okay, now I need to lift you. It might hurt, but I'll try to be careful."

The dog thumped his tail against the snow twice but otherwise stayed perfectly still. I slowly lifted him into my arms, then started back to the Jeep. When I got there, I opened the tailgate. The dog in my arms began to squirm when he saw Tilly.

"Get in front, Tilly," I instructed.

Tilly crawled through the opening between the driver's and passenger seats, then made herself comfortable on the latter. I gently laid the injured dog on the floor in the cargo area, closed the tailgate, and headed around to the driver's side door. I drove as quickly as I could safely. When I reached Brady's the clinic was dark, so I went up to the front door and rang the bell. I could hear laughter coming from inside; I assumed both Brady and Lilly were home.

"Tess, what are you doing here?" Brady asked. "Is Tilly okay?"

"She's fine. I found a dog on the side of the road. He appears to have a broken leg. I think he must have been hit by a car."

"Okay, let's take a look."

Brady followed me out to the Jeep. I lifted the tailgate and Brady leaned inside. As I had, Brady spoke to the dog in a quiet, soothing tone of voice. After a moment he picked up the dog, and Tilly and I followed them into the clinic.

"So?" I asked.

"The leg is definitely broken. I think he has a couple of broken ribs as well. I'll need to take some X-rays. He doesn't have a collar. Have you ever seen him before?"

"No, never."

Brady took out his stethoscope and listened to the dog's heart and breathing. "I'm concerned there could be a small tear in the lung. I'll know more after the X-ray. You can either wait or leave him."

"I'll wait."

Brady pushed the table the dog was lying on into the back room, where the X-ray machine and the surgical equipment were kept. I took the opportunity to call Tony to let him know I wasn't going to make it with dinner after all. I wanted to hear what he had to say, so I told him I'd call him again when I got home.

Several minutes later, Brady joined me where I was waiting. "I've given him some light sedation. Thankfully, the lungs are fine, but the leg will need to be set, and he does have a couple of cracked ribs. The leg is broken in several places, but I think it will be fine in the long run. I'll keep the dog here for a few days until I'm sure there aren't any hidden injuries. If you do manage to track down the owner, let me know. I'll put a photo of him on my website as well."

"Thanks, Brady. The poor little guy. I feel so bad for him. Whoever hit him just left him there to die."

"He's lucky you found him. He wouldn't have made it through the night if you hadn't."

"I'm always happy to do anything I can for any animal in need."

"That reminds me, I wanted to thank you again for helping out on Saturday. The adoption clinic was more successful than I even hoped."

"We had a lot of awesome volunteers and we managed to find a lot of dogs really good homes."

"We did have a lot of good volunteers, but I watched you and noticed you went above and beyond to make sure every dog found the perfect home. I'd like to take you to dinner to thank you."

I smiled. "That would be nice, but it really isn't necessary."

"Nonsense. Lilly and I are having dinner tomorrow with an old school friend. How about Wednesday night?"

"Wednesday is Valentine's Day."

Brady clicked his fingers. "That's right; I forgot. I'm sure you have plans with your special someone."

"Actually, I don't have plans on Wednesday. I guess I just assumed you and Lilly might be doing something."

"Lilly and I are just friends."

"Okay, then if the Valentine thing doesn't make it weird for you, I'd love to have dinner with you on Wednesday."

Brady smiled. "Great. I'll pick you up at your place at seven."

"Great. I'm looking forward to it." I glanced toward the door. "I should be on my way."

"Before you go, how's Bruiser doing with Hattie?"

"They seem to be getting along really well. Hattie did say he seemed to hate Hap, but I suspect it was the hugging and physical contact between them he didn't like. When I delivered his mail today, I suggested he give Bruiser some space until he gets to know him better. Hap will be having dinner at Hattie's for Valentine's Day on Wednesday, so he plans to bring a pocketful of dog treats with him."

"Hap seems to be a patient guy; I think things will be fine."

Chapter 11

I headed home with Tilly from the clinic. I was anxious to hear what Tony had found out about Danko and Maria Milovich and Romero Montenegro. I was sorry our dinner hadn't worked out, but I'd had several late nights in a row, so the idea of turning in early wasn't a bad one. At home, I fed Tilly and the kittens, then changed into an old pair of sweatpants and a long-sleeved T-shirt that had once been Mike's but I'd somehow ended up with. I put a bowl of soup in the microwave, then clicked on my computer and waited for it to boot up. I figured I'd eat first, then call Tony. Our conversation had the potential to be a lengthy one and I didn't want to be interrupted until we were finished.

When the soup was ready, I poured myself a glass of wine and sat down in front of the computer to eat and check my emails. Most of what I had was junk, but there was an email from an old high school friend, letting me know she'd be in town next month and wanting to arrange to get together, and another from one of the women I'd helped at the adoption clinic, saying how happy she was with the new best friend she'd adopted. I was about to log off when my phone rang. I thought it might be Tony calling because he'd grown tired of waiting for me to get in touch, but instead I was greeted by a deep voice that said, "It will be best for everyone if you leave things alone." The connection clicked off.

"What the...?" I asked no one in particular. I looked at the caller ID, but all it said was *caller unknown*. I figured if someone had gone to the trouble to call me, I must be getting close to something someone didn't want me to know. The question was, which mystery was the caller associated with, and what didn't he want me to find?

I called Tony to see if he had any idea what was behind the mysterious call. He'd been digging around in several areas on my behalf; maybe someone had found out and wasn't happy about it. "I just got the strangest call," I said as soon as he picked up, then explained what had been said.

"I don't like the sound of that," Tony said. "Maybe you should come over here after all. Plan to spend the night. I'd come to you, but I have a better security system here."

I hesitated. The call had freaked me out, but staying with Tony would add a good twenty minutes to my commute in the morning, and unless we were able to figure out who'd called me and were able to deal with him, the threat of someone intruding on my space would be fairly open-ended.

"No," I said. "I appreciate the offer, but I didn't get the feeling I was in any immediate danger, and spending the night at your place tonight would only be a temporary solution. Tomorrow night I'll be right back here in the same boat. I think the better move is to get these mysteries wrapped up."

"Whatever you think is best, but my invitation is open, if you decide you aren't comfortable alone."

"I'm not alone. I have Tilly, Tangletoe, and Tinder to protect me if need be."

Tony chuckled. "Yes, I'm sure they're quite the bodyguards."

"As long as I have you on the phone, I want to ask about the searches you've been conducting for me."

"Okay. First off, Romero Montenegro seems legit. His family owns a large vineyard in northern Italy, which is where he grew up. He used to work in a museum but currently teaches history at a university in Rome. I noticed he's on sabbatical until next fall, which probably accounts for his being in the States. He's never been married or arrested, though he did have one failed engagement seven years ago. I dug around pretty deep, and I think he's probably a nice guy who met and developed a friendship with an older woman."

"Older? How much older?"

"How old is your mother?" Tony asked.

"Fifty-six."

"Montenegro is forty-two."

"Why would a forty-two-year-old man be interested in a fifty-six-year-old woman?"

"Your mother is bright, intelligent, and funny. She's also very beautiful."

I frowned. "It almost sounds like you have a thing for her."

"I don't, but I can appreciate the fact that she has a lot to offer a man. Montenegro seems okay. He's making your mother happy. If I were you, I wouldn't do anything to mess that up."

"Yeah, okay. I guess I feel better about him hanging out with my mother after what you've found. Places like museums and universities usually conduct background checks before hiring new personnel, so chances are he doesn't have any awful skeletons in his closet. What did you find out about Danko Milovich?"

"As we know, he's a very wealthy businessman. What we didn't know is that he lives in Serbia. And it appears he's influential as well as rich. He met and married an American named Maria Worthington while living in Washington, DC, in 1982. From what I can tell, Milovich had plans to go back to Serbia during the summer of 1983, but Maria disappeared in June, just weeks before they were to leave America. Milovich remained in the States for an additional six months while an extensive search for his missing wife was conducted. In January of 1984 he gave up his search and returned to his homeland."

"I wonder why Maria fled."

"I can't be sure," Tony answered, "but it sounds as if Milovich is unyielding as well as rich and powerful. He's known for running his businesses with an iron fist. He probably ran his home in the same manner."

"Maybe Maria found out she was pregnant and didn't want to raise her baby in Serbia, where she'd have little recourse if things at home became unbearable."

"Perhaps. From what I can tell, Milovich continued to look for Maria for years, even after he returned to Serbia."

"It sounds like she got away from the monster she was married to only to have our investigation on Coby's behalf add fuel to a fire that had all but died."

"That seems to be the case," Tony agreed.

I sat down on the sofa and let Tinder crawl into my lap. "So what do we do? Do we stop looking for her in the hope that her husband will stop looking too, or do we continue the search, so we can warn her that her husband might be looking for her again?"

"I'm not sure. I do think we need to talk to Coby to tell him what we've learned. The fact that one of Milovich's employees followed Coby to White Eagle indicates to me that he knows or at least suspects Coby is his son. Either that or he knows Coby has a photo of Maria and is looking for her. He could be in danger."

"I agree; we have to tell Coby. I'll call him to see if he wants to meet me at Sisters' for breakfast tomorrow. You're welcome to come as well if you can make it into town by seven-thirty."

"I'll be there. In the meantime, I'll take another look to see if I can pick up Maria's trail after she left here. Knowing where she's been could help to narrow down where she is now."

"I want to help Coby find his mother, but I'm worried all we're doing is leading her husband, who she clearly doesn't want to have anything to do with, directly to her. What if he finds her because of our investigation and ends up hurting her or worse?"

"That's an argument we need to make with Coby when we see him. He seems to care about her. I think once he has all the pieces of the puzzle, he'll realize on his own that not finding Maria might be the best thing for them both."

Chapter 12

Tuesday, February 13

Tony arrived at Sisters' Diner at the same time Tilly and I did, so we went ahead and took the large booth in the back. We were a few minutes early; Coby would probably arrive soon.

"Anymore weird calls?" Tony asked after we got settled.

"No, just the one. The thing is, I'm not even sure what the caller wants me to leave alone. The search for Daisy or the search for my father?"

"I suppose either situation has the potential to turn into something pretty explosive. In both circumstances, an individual chose to disappear. I guess we should assume both Maria and your father had a good reason for doing so."

"I can understand why Maria would want to run away if she feared for her baby and herself, but I can't imagine why my father would have chosen to leave us the way he did. Still, if Grant Thomas faked his own death and disappeared, as we suspect, he must have had a reason for going to such extreme measures."

"The phone call you received is likely the result of our digging around in something someone doesn't want revealed. Do you think we should stop?" Tony asked.

"As far as my search for my dad goes, no, I don't plan to stop until I have my answers." I glanced toward the front door and waved. "When it comes to our search for Maria, we'll tell Coby what we found out about the woman we're fairly certain is his mother and see what he wants to do."

Once Coby arrived, my mom came over and we placed our order. I wasn't sure how I felt about the glow in her cheeks and the twinkle in her eye. Don't get me wrong, I want my mother to be happy, I just wasn't sure how I felt about the young, good-looking Italian who was making her that way.

"Okay, what did you find?" Coby asked as soon as my mother walked away.

Tony explained about the men who had been waiting for him at his house, as well as the information he'd been able to dig up about Danko and Maria Milovich.

"So you think the woman I suspect is my mother was married to this Serbian businessman?" Coby clarified.

"That's our assumption," I answered.

Coby frowned. "And if all our assumptions are true, that man is my father?"

"It would seem," I confirmed.

Coby sat back in the booth without speaking. I watched as varying emotions were displayed on his face as he struggled to work things out in his mind. "So, what it looks like is that she ran away after she found out she was pregnant with me. She was so concerned that my father might find me that she abandoned me in a church and cut all ties between herself and her baby. Thirty-four years later, her grown son is so curious about the woman in the photo that was left with him when he was abandoned that he decides to search for her. That search, as it turns out, could very well lead the man his mother ran from all those years ago back to her."

"There's some supposition in the scenario you outlined, but yes, I believe our search could potentially lead Milovich to the woman who's been hiding from him for over three decades," I replied.

Coby leaned forward, took a sip of his coffee, and began drumming his fingers on the table in front of him. "What do I do? Do I stop my search to protect my mother, or is it already too late for that? Might our search have provided my father a strong enough lead that he'll be able to track her down on his own? And if that's possible, should we continue to look for her so we can warn her?"

Neither Tony nor I spoke right away. It was such a tricky situation, I was pretty sure neither of us wanted to give Coby bad advice.

Eventually, Tony said, "Milovich's employee knew you were looking for Maria, but I have no idea how Milovich found out *I* was looking for Maria. My first thought was that he'd set up an alarm to notify him if anyone did a background search or ran a facial recognition program like the one I've been using, but

I have my own protection set up to deal with that possibility, and I can assure you, my computer system hasn't been accessed by anyone but me."

"So how did he find out you're helping Coby look for Maria?" I asked.

"I suppose Milovich might have someone in White Eagle who might know we're working together. Now that I think about it, it makes sense he would send someone else after Kowalski died."

"I think we should continue looking for my mother so we can find her and warn her," Coby said decisively.

I nodded. "Okay. We'll keep looking."

When I left the restaurant, Tony and Coby were still discussing possible ways of addressing the current situation, and I hoped by the time they went their separate ways they'd come up with a plan. I was almost ten minutes late picking up my mailbags, but Queenie didn't say anything about my tardiness, so neither did I. I made good time during the first two hours of my route until I got to the Book Boutique, where Bree was waiting for me.

"I got another gift from my mystery man," she said with a huge smile on her face.

"What'd he send today?"

"A dozen heart-shaped sugar cookies. They're really good. Try one."

I frowned as I looked in to the box. The cookies were decorated with red frosting and white sprinkles. Mike was Bree's mystery man?

"Is something wrong?" Bree asked.

"No. I'm fine."

"You have a scowl on your face."

I offered Bree a smile. "Sorry. I was just debating whether to take you up on your offer of a cookie. Normally, I would, but I had breakfast with Tony and Coby, so I think I'll pass."

"Coby really is the nicest guy. I know he's only in town for another week or so, but I've very much enjoyed his company. Most guys who want to spend time with me are only after one thing, but Coby is happy for us to hang out as friends. We're even going to go out tomorrow night for a Valenfriend Day dinner."

"It looks like we're both in the friend zone this year. I have a date with Brady tomorrow night, although he's taking me out to thank me for helping at the clinic and has nothing to do with romance."

"We should double," Bree suggested. "I'm sure the guys won't mind if neither has romance on his mind."

"That's a good idea. I'll mention it to Brady and let you know. I need to get going. I'll call you later."

I headed directly to the sheriff's office. "Is Mike in his office?" I asked Frank.

"He is."

"I need to talk to him, but I'm going to leave Tilly with you."

I told Tilly to stay, then went down the hall. Mike was working on his computer when I arrived. I stepped into his office and closed the door behind me. "You're Bree's secret Valentine," I accused.

Mike frowned. "How did you find out?"

I sat down in the chair across from him. "I have my ways. What I really want to ask is why? Are you interested in Bree? Romantically, I mean."

"No. You and Bree have been friends since you were in preschool. I care about her, but not in that way."

"So why the gifts?"

"Guilt."

I raised a brow. "Would you care to elaborate?"

"Bree came to see me after I arrested Donny. I had reason to suspect him of Pike's death, but she was so angry with me. For the first time in my life I felt hatred coming at me from a person I considered almost family."

"You were just doing your job," I pointed out.

"I know. And I'd do it again. But when Donny went to prison, Bree was so depressed. It was like the light I'd always associated with her was extinguished. I was at the bookstore last week and we got to talking while she rang up my books. She seemed so sad, and when I asked her what was wrong, she told me how upset she was with her complete lack of a love life with Valentine's Day just around the corner. On impulse, I sent her flowers. I wanted to cheer her up, but I didn't want things to be weird between us, so I sent them anonymously."

"That was very nice, and the flowers really did cheer her up, but why did you continue with the other gifts?"

Mike shrugged. "I'm not sure. I never intended to have the secret Valentine thing become a big deal, but when I ran into her the day after I sent the flowers, she was so happy. I'd been feeling bad about the role I played in everything that had happened to cause her depression in the first place that her smile made me feel as though a weight had been lifted from me. I saw the chocolates and sent them, and I guess you know the rest."

"Are you going to tell her that you're the one who's been sending the gifts?"

Mike shook his head. "No. And you aren't going to either. Bree is happy with the mystery and romance of it all. Her smile has returned, which was my goal all along. She'll receive a card with movie tickets in it tomorrow and that will be it. The Valentine mystery will naturally come to an end, and she never needs to know who was behind it."

I had to agree it would probably be better for Bree not to know it had been Mike who'd sent her the gifts. She was imagining Prince Charming. It seemed best to leave her with that image in her mind, so I promised Mike I'd keep his secret.

Chapter 13

Between the late start and the side trip to see Mike, I was going to really need to hustle to finish my route on time. Fortunately, the shops in town were busy, so most of the folks I normally stopped to chat with were dealing with customers when I stopped by. I was just tossing my empty mailbag into the Jeep when my phone pinged, letting me know I had a text. It was from Tony, to say he had news. I texted back that I needed to stop off at the post office and then I was heading home. He responded to say he'd meet me at my cabin.

When I got home, Tony's truck was already in my drive. I pulled up and parked before opening the tailgate for Tilly, who jumped down and greeted Tony and Titan. Both dogs trotted to the front door.

"You brought pizza," I said, noticing the box in his hand.

"And beer," he added, holding up a brown paper bag.

"I feel like we've been having a lot of beer and pizza lately."

"I like beer and pizza."

I grinned. "So do I. In fact, if I had to choose just one meal to eat for the rest of my life, it would be beer and pizza." I unlocked the door and was greeted by two rambunctious kittens, who seemed happy to finally have someone home. "I'm going to change my clothes real fast and then we can eat and talk." I went to my bedroom while Tony fed the animals. I pulled on a pair of overly large sweatpants and a long-sleeved T-shirt, then joined him in the kitchen.

"What's so important you had to drive all the way over here to talk to me?" I asked.

Tony picked up a large slice of the cheesy pie and slipped it onto his plate. "After you left this morning, Coby and I discussed ways we could continue to look for his mother while staying off his father's radar, if in fact that's who they are. After a bit we realized if Maria Worthington and Daisy are the same person, we might be able to track her down via the Worthington family."

"Do you think she kept in touch with them?"

"I wasn't sure, but I figured it was worth a try. I did a little research and found out Maria's parents died when she was a young woman, but she had a sister, Veronica, who's married to a man named Daniel Portland. I tracked her to her last known address, in Denver. Unfortunately, she'd moved, but I'm pretty sure I've found her. I'm waiting for confirmation, but it appears she divorced Portland in 1998 and moved to Seattle, where she met and married a man named Elon Ramsey."

"Does she still live in Seattle?" I asked.

"If my trail isn't flawed, I think she does. I have a contact at the DMV who's verifying that the present Veronica Ramsey is the same person who was once married to Daniel Portland."

"Do you think she'll know where Maria is?"

Tony took a bite of his pizza, chewed, and swallowed. "Honestly, I'm not sure. It's worth a conversation to find out. When I hear back from my buddy at the DMV, we can decide how best to follow up with Veronica."

I looked at Tony with what I was sure was an expression of suspicion. "Is there something else? It seems to me that you could easily have told me what you just did over the phone."

Tony took a sip of his beer, then set aside the bottle. "There is something else. It has to do with your dad."

Okay, that got my attention. "So spill. What did you find out?"

"The photo of Jared Collins that appears to have been taken in Norway was part of a surveillance report conducted by a private investigator working for a state senator named Galvin Kline. I'm not sure exactly why Kline was having Collins watched, but I traced the photo back to the PI who took it and was able to find additional photos of the same man taken during the midseventies. Based on those photos, it appears Collins got around. I managed to locate photos of him in Paris, London, Belfast, Tokyo, and several other cities in Europe and Asia."

"So if Collins and my dad are the same person, he traveled extensively, not just to Norway. Why would he lie about that? It isn't even that he lied; he went out of his way to say on several different occasions I can remember that while he'd been to every one of the continental United States, he'd never traveled to a foreign country."

"I don't have answers for that," Tony answered. "Keep in mind, what I pulled up was a travel history relating to Jared Collins. We still haven't definitively proven Jared Collins and Grant Thomas are the same person, though I'll say that from the additional photos, my level of confidence that they're of the same man has increased significantly. If your mom has a photo of your father when he was in his early twenties, we'd know more. But even if we do find proof that Jared Collins and Grant Thomas are the same person, it won't tell us where he is now or why he faked his own death."

I sat back in my chair, peeling away the label on my beer bottle as I tried to digest Tony's words. If Jared Collins was Grant Thomas, he must have decided to leave his old life behind and take on a new persona, that of a small-town, cross-country trucker. But why? Was he a spy? A fugitive? Could he have been in witness protection, or was he a member of some secret group or international order? So many questions needing answers.

"What do we do now?" I asked.

"I think you need to find an opportunity to ask your mom about the photos and I'll keep digging. Keep in mind, digging could be dangerous. We still don't know if the threatening call you received was a reaction to our search for Maria Milovich or Grant Thomas. I want to help you find your answers, but I don't want you to be in danger because of our snooping around."

I pushed my beer bottle toward the center of the table, then leaned forward. "I know I'm taking a risk digging into all this, but I need to know. One way or another, I need to understand why my father made the decisions he did."

"Okay. I'll do what I can to help you find your answers, but you have to promise that if you get anymore creepy phone calls, you'll tell me. I'd never be able to live with myself if my investigating caused you harm in any way."

"I'll tell you if I get any additional calls. It's not like I'm looking for danger."

Tony picked up his phone. "There's a text from my contact. He confirms Veronica Ramsey is the sister of Maria Milovich."

"So, do we call her?"

Tony didn't answer right away; I could tell he was thinking things over. "I think we should have Coby contact her, nephew to aunt."

"That's a good idea. I'll call him to see if he's free to come over."

******

Tony tracked down a cell number for Veronica. When Coby arrived, we helped him write a text to her.

"We don't know if she even knew her sister had a baby," I said. "The text should include a brief history of where you were found and the photo that was found with you," I began.

"It's probably okay to say you were abandoned in a church, but I wouldn't mention White Eagle just

131

yet," Tony said. "It's possible her sympathy might be with the abandoned husband."

Tony had a point. "Maybe you should just say you were adopted and have been searching for your birth mother and have reason to believe it may be Maria," I suggested. "You can always add details if she's responsive to speaking to you."

"I'll speak from the heart but keep things vague for now," Coby agreed. "Is there anything I should add?"

"Maybe include a phone number and an email address where she can get in touch with you," I said.

Coby did as I suggested. "I'm really nervous," he said. "What if she isn't interested in talking to me?"

"What aunt wouldn't want to connect with a long-lost nephew she might not have even known existed?" I asked.

Coby received a reply a few minutes later: *I don't know where Maria is. Don't contact me again.*

******

Later that evening, I tossed a log on the fire, poured myself a glass of wine, and sat down on the sofa with a quilt, my kittens, and the sketchbook I'd taken from the Honeycutt house. I didn't expect to find the answers we were looking for in it, but I was too wound up to go to bed, and I hadn't had a chance to look through it yet. The sketches were quite good. I recognized many as locations around town, so the person it belonged to must either have lived in the area or stayed here for a significant amount of time. About halfway through the book, I found a sketch of a woman who looked a lot like Maria, sitting on a rock. The detail the artist had included was remarkable.

I continued to look though the book, finding quite a few additional sketches of Maria posing in front of different backdrops. All of them looked to have been drawn at the Honeycutt house, including several of Maria sitting on the porch rocking on the swing or sitting on the stoop. If I had to guess, the artist and Maria had spent quite a bit of time together during her stay in White Eagle.

The longer I stared at the sketches, the more certain I became that something wasn't right. On the surface, it seemed we'd most likely figured out what had happened. Maria had married a rich, powerful man only to find that, like many rich, powerful men, he had a cruel side. Maria learned she was pregnant right about the time her husband announced plans to move back to his home country. Not wanting her child to be brought up there, she fled. At some point she met Edith Honeycutt, who'd provided her with a place to hide out until the baby was born. Then she wrapped her newborn in a blanket, went to Kalispell, and left the baby in the church. Perhaps at the last minute she left a photo of herself with him, needing to provide some connection between herself and her son. Then she disappeared, apparently never to be seen again.

Thirty-four years later, a dying man gave the photo to his son on his deathbed. The woman in the photo is assumed to be the biological mother of the man's adopted son. The son decides to find her, only to run into one roadblock after another. When he questioned the parishioners at the church in Kalispell, no one remembered a baby ever being left in the church. If the baby had been left anonymously, wouldn't some effort have been made to identify the parents of the child? Wouldn't someone remember this, even if no one had seen the mother?

And then there was the fact that a man who had a photo of Coby in his glove box happened to become involved in a fatal accident with the man he was following. I mean really, what were the odds of that happening?

Tilly came over and put her paw on my leg, which was her way of letting me know she was ready to go to bed. I set the sketchbook aside, then let her out for a quick bathroom break while I washed up and changed into my pajamas. After I let Tilly back in, the four residents of the cabin headed into the bedroom and cozied up in bed.

Chapter 14

Wednesday, February 14

It snowed overnight, but the sun was shining brightly by the time Tilly and I went into work. I was looking forward to dinner with Brady, Bree, and Coby, and made a personal commitment to get my route done in a timely manner so I'd have plenty of time to get ready. Technically, my dinner with Brady wasn't a date. We were going out as friends, but he was picking me up *and* paying, so I decided to let myself refer to the evening as one, despite the fact that exhibits of intimacy would most likely not be part of the package.

"Good morning, Queenie," I greeted her when Tilly and I arrived at the post office. "Another two-bagger today?"

"No. I guess folks were organized this year and made sure their cards were delivered before the holiday. Do you have plans tonight?"

"Yes, I do," I answered as I slipped my bag onto my shoulder.

"I don't suppose your plans would include that handsome young man you've been hanging around with for the past week?"

"If you mean Coby, no. At least not directly. Brady Baker and I are going out to dinner with Bree and Coby. It's really more of a friends thing than a date thing, but I'm excited about it."

"Sounds like a fun group."

"I think it will be. I even have a new dress for the occasion. At first, I wasn't going to go to any special effort because my Valentine's dinner isn't really a date, but at the last minute I bought that strapless red dress that's been in Hannigan's window all month. They only had one left, but it was my size and fits perfectly."

"I know the dress you mean. It's a beautiful dress, but I'm betting it cost more than you make in a week. Seems pretty special for a dinner that's not a date."

I shrugged. "Yeah, I guess it does, but you know Bree will wear something gorgeous. I've never been able to compete with her because she looks absolutely perfect with seemingly no effort, but I want to look nice tonight too."

"You always look nice, darling, even when you're wearing faded jeans and that old red sweatshirt. But I get what you mean. I have a couple of friends who make beautiful look effortless as well. Best get going so you have time to do your hair and makeup."

"I'm gone. I'll see you this afternoon." I headed to the door leading out to the parking area, where I'd left my Jeep. Tilly followed closely behind. With any luck, we'd have the route done in record time, leaving plenty of time for primping before Brady picked me up.

Of course, as usual, things didn't quite work out as I planned.

******

"What do you mean, Armand Kowalski was murdered? I thought he had a heart attack."

"He did have a heart attack," Mike answered. I plastered my cell phone to my ear and waited for him to continue. "But it didn't occur naturally."

I narrowed my gaze and looked up to the sky, which was filled with snow flurries. This conversation wasn't making a bit of sense. I was less than a quarter mile from Mike's office, so I told him I'd be right over to talk in person. I hung up and began to walk quickly down the sidewalk with Tilly trotting along beside me. I couldn't know for certain at this point, but I had the feeling this surprising twist was going to interfere with the perfectly lovely evening I had planned.

"Okay, catch me up," I said to Mike as soon as Tilly and I entered his office.

"I just received Kowalski's full autopsy report. While the cause of death was heart failure, the medical examiner found a large quantity of Jax in Kowalski's system."

"What's Jax?"

"A synthetically produced street drug. It's usually sold as a powder, and when used in small doses, snorting it can create a feeling of euphoria. The Jax found in Kowalski's body wasn't powder but the liquid form of the drug. Liquid Jax can kill you, and a large quantity can do it in less than a minute."

"So why are you just learning about this now?"

"Jax isn't widely available or widely used, so it isn't one of the drugs tested for in a standard tox screen. The ME found a small puncture wound in the victim's chest, so he ordered a full tox screen. It appears the drug was injected directly into his heart. He would have been dead within seconds."

I took off my bag and sat down on the chair across from Mike's desk. It appeared this wasn't going to be a quick conversation. "Okay, say this actually happened. Say someone injected Kowalski with this drug. Who could have done such a thing? There was no one around other than me and Coby."

Mike raised one brow. "What exactly do you know about this Coby Walters?"

"I know he's a nice guy who's in town to find his biological mother. Yes, he was involved in the accident in which Kowalski died, but he didn't kill him. He tried to save him. I personally watched him give him CPR."

"Seems if I had just killed a man and there was a witness at the scene, I might try giving him CPR to make it look like I was trying to save his life instead."

I closed my eyes tight against the imagery Mike's statement had created. I swallowed hard and opened them again. "Are you saying Coby first injected Kowalski with a lethal dose of a street drug and then gave him CPR knowing he was already dead?"

"I believe that's exactly what I just said."

"But why? Why would Coby kill him?"

"I don't know for certain, but the man did have a photo of Coby in his glove box. We've since learned Kowalski worked for the man we're assuming is Coby's biological father."

"Yeah, but Coby didn't know about any of that at the time of the accident."

Mike sat forward and entwined his hands on the desk in front of him. "Didn't he?"

"How could he?"

"I haven't figure it all out yet, but it's beginning to look like things may not be exactly as they seem."

I leaned my head back and closed my eyes. This couldn't be happening. After a few seconds I opened my eyes and sat slightly forward. "Okay, say Coby knew Kowalski was following him. For things to have gone down the way you suggest, Coby would have had to have been traveling with a syringe filled with Jax. That doesn't make sense. He had no way to predict the accident would even occur."

"Unless it wasn't an accident."

I tilted my head back once again, only this time I looked up at the ceiling. Coby a killer? Mike had to be wrong. I lowered my head and looked at my brother once again. "Is there any scenario other than Coby as the killer in which the man who died could have been injected with the drug?"

"I guess you could have done it."

I rolled my eyes. "I didn't, so let's move on. Maybe there was someone else in the car Kowalski was driving. Maybe after the accident occurred the person traveling with Kowalski somehow stuck the syringe in his chest, got out of the car, and took off into the woods."

"Did you see any evidence of a passenger?"

"No," I admitted.

"Footprints in the snow? Anything at all?"

"No," I groaned.

"And didn't you tell me the side of the car was buckled so the door wouldn't open, so you had to break the back window and get Kowalski out that way?"

I sighed. "Yes, I did say that."

"You also said Kowalski was unconscious when you found him. Probably from the head wound. Was Coby alone with the man at any point?"

I cringed. "Yes. After we broke the back window and he crawled inside, he sent me back up to my Jeep to get a blanket. When I got back, he said the man wasn't breathing." Oh God. It really did look like Coby had killed Kowalski. "Did you bring him in?"

"I tried, but we've been unable to locate him. We checked with the employees at the Inn. They said he had breakfast and lunch with everyone else but left shortly after that. He told one of the other guests he had a date."

"Bree!" I shouted. "His date is with Bree."

Mike stood up. "I'm going to the bookstore. Try to call her."

Mike hurried out the office door while I called the bookstore. There was no answer. I called her house. No answer there either. I left messages in both places, and then Tilly and I followed Mike down the street. If Coby had killed Kowalski and he'd somehow found out Mike was on to him, Bree could be in real trouble if she was with him.

When I arrived at the bookstore, it was dark inside. There was a note on the door letting customers know Bree had closed early for Valentine's Day. Mike was on the phone, but he hung up shortly after I got there.

"I'm going to look for Bree," Mike said. "You call Tony. Have him dig around to see what he can find out about Coby, Kowalski, and the woman who's supposedly Coby's mother."

"Okay. I'll call him. You have to find her."

"I will."

I called Tony and quickly explained what was going on. He told me that he'd found some irregularities and had planned to call me anyway. He asked me to come to his place and I said I would. What I really wanted to do was go look for Bree, but if she wasn't at the bookstore or at home, I had no idea where to look. My best bet was with the man who seemed to have a knack for pulling a rabbit out of his hat just when you needed it most.

By the time Tilly and I arrived at Tony's, it was getting dark. I realized I'd never finished my route; my bag was back in Mike's office. The mail within would have to wait. I called Queenie to explain what had happened so she wouldn't worry, then called Brady to cancel our date. I felt bad for doing it at the last minute, but he didn't sound like he minded in the least. In fact, if you asked me, he sounded almost relieved. I supposed after he'd thought about things, he'd realized dinner with a friend wasn't the sort of thing you did on Valentine's Day if you had no desire for that person to be anything more than a friend.

I hung up with Brady and called Mike's cell, who confirmed Bree definitely wasn't at her house.

"Okay, what do we know?" I asked Tony after I put away my cell phone.

He took me by the hand and led me into his computer room, pointed to a seat, and began to speak. "I'm going to throw a lot of information at you really fast. If you aren't following, stop me."

"Okay. What's going on?"

"I decided to call the man who'd been waiting for us in the Suburban; the one who left me his business card. I hoped he would be willing to fill in a few of the blanks we hadn't been able to do on our own."

"Why would you think he'd tell us anything?"

"I didn't have any reason to think he would, but it seemed he wanted to find Maria as much as we did, so I figured calling him couldn't hurt."

"He could have turned it around and used the conversation to get information out of you," I pointed out.

"He could have, but we didn't actually know anything about where Maria might be."

"Yeah, I guess that's true. So how did it go?"

"Once again, he told me that he worked for Maria's husband, Danko Milovich. He assured me that he meant Maria no harm and that his dictate from his boss was simply to protect her."

I frowned. "Did you believe him?"

"Not at first. But he seemed to be willing to talk, so I decided to play things out to see where they went. I asked him how he knew I'd been looking for Maria, and he said one of his men had been following a man who claimed to be Maria's biological child."

"Kowalski?"

"Yes. According to the man I spoke to, whose name is Dracon, both he and Kowalski had been hired to protect Maria. When she decided to come to the States, they, along with a third man named Borden, came with her."

I held up my hand. "Whoa, back up. What do you mean, she decided to come to the States?"

"Maria had been living in Serbia with her husband until two months ago, when she received a message from a friend in the United States that a man claiming to be her son was looking for her. She'd always wondered what had become of the child, so she made a trip back to the States to check it out. She knew her husband would never let her return on her own, but he was away on business, so she took advantage of it and made travel arrangements. It seems Dracon, Kowalski, and Borden were hired many years ago by Milovich to act as bodyguards for his wife, so Maria had no choice but to let them come with her. If she'd refused, they would have contacted her husband about her plans."

"Okay, I'm following so far, but why all the security? Three men to protect one woman? Were they afraid she would run away again?"

"According to Dracon, there'd been a kidnapping attempt involving Maria when they lived here before. It seems Milovich has enemies who will do almost anything to gain leverage against him."

"You said the kidnapping occurred when he lived in the United States. That must have been in the early eighties, when Milovich first met and married Maria."

"Exactly. After the kidnapping attempt, Milovich decided to move back to Serbia. At about that same time, Maria found out she was pregnant. She loved her husband and intended to do what was necessary to protect herself from her husband's enemies, but she didn't want her baby to grow up in such a dangerous and restrictive environment. She knew as Danko's son, his freedom would be limited, and she wanted him to have a normal life. A life like the one she'd enjoyed before marrying Milovich."

"Okay, so Maria found out she was pregnant and decided she didn't want her baby to be raised in Serbia, so she ran?"

"Basically," Tony confirmed. "Somehow, she managed to give her bodyguard the slip and took off in the middle of the night. She acted rashly, because she didn't have a plan or any money or means of support, but she was lucky enough to meet Edith her first day on her own. Edith took her in and hid her from everyone who was looking for her. After the baby was born, Edith promised to find a good home for her son, so Maria left her baby with her and went back to her husband."

"So the whole church thing was a lie?"

"Yes. It was part of the story Coby made up. In reality, Edith had placed Maria's son with a family she knew who very much wanted children but were unable to have any of their own."

"If Maria went home after the baby was born, wouldn't her husband wonder what had become of him and use his resources to find the child?"

"It seems Maria hadn't told her husband she was pregnant. He managed to find it out on his own, but at the time of Maria's disappearance, he was unaware of the pregnancy."

I took a moment to work through everything Tony had just told me. In a really twisted way, the whole thing made sense, but I was having trouble fast-forwarding from Maria giving birth and going home to the present day. "Okay, so Kowalski was following Coby because he was looking for Maria."

"Correct. After Maria left for the States, her husband called home. It was at that point that he found out his wife had left on a trip to find her long-lost son. Milovich checked in with Maria's security detail, only to find she had given them the slip. They were looking for her by then and had learned Coby was looking for her as well. Milovich knew right away Coby wasn't the son his wife had given birth to, knew he most likely wanted to find Maria to harm her in some way, so he ordered Maria's security detail to follow Coby."

"How did Milovich know Coby wasn't Maria's son?"

"Apparently, Milovich had known where the boy was for quite some time. He knew it was important to Maria that their child have a normal life, so he allowed the boy to be raised by the family Edith had found, but he'd been keeping an eye on him from a distance."

I leaned forward, rested my elbows on my thighs, then bowed my head into my hands. "If Coby isn't Maria's son, who is he and why is he looking for her?"

"Dracon believes he's looking for her for the same reason the men who tried to kidnap her thirty-four years ago did: leverage. Milovich is not only wealthy, he's powerful. In his own country he's untouchable. Dracon believes the man we know as Coby was hired to kidnap Maria."

"They want to ransom her?" I asked.

"Dracon suggested the plot involves more than money, that whoever hired Coby needs something

Milovich has and is determined to acquire it by any means. He wouldn't go into specifics, but he assured me that getting hold of the one thing Milovich cares about is the only way to get to him."

I leaned back against the sofa and stared at the ceiling. "So Coby's been lying to us the whole time."

"I'm afraid so. He realized we might be helpful in his search for Milovich's wife, so he made up a very compelling story and asked for our help."

"I'm such an idiot."

"You're not an idiot. Coby had us all fooled."

I glanced at Tony. "We need to find Bree."

"I know. I'm working on it."

I called Mike, who still hadn't found either Bree or Coby. He promised to keep looking and I promised to stay in touch. What I needed was one of those lightbulb moments when everything that hadn't made sense suddenly did. I needed to quell my emotions and think rationally. Tony was working on his computer, so at first, the only thing I could do was pace. Everyone knew that in tense situations where everything was on the line, someone always paced.

I took a deep breath and tried to focus my thoughts. It seemed Coby was looking for Maria to kidnap her. We suspected he was working with one of Milovich's enemies and that he had lured her to the United States by masquerading as her son. She had arrived with three bodyguards in tow but had managed to ditch them at some point. The last time I'd seen Coby he hadn't found her, which meant she was in hiding. Maybe she wanted to be sure she'd lost her bodyguards, or maybe she was just being cautious and was trying to get more information on Coby before she approached him. The question was, where would she go?

I didn't think I had enough information to figure that out, so I turned my thoughts to Bree. Coby had been hanging out with us all week. He'd arranged to take her out for Valentine's Day. If Coby didn't know we were on to him, she could be totally safe. Even if they were together, as I suspected, that didn't mean they weren't simply engaged in datelike activities until it was time to meet Brady and me at the restaurant. I needed to hang on to that thought; otherwise I was going to flip out completely.

"Bree and Coby were in the liquor store just north of town at four-thirty," Tony said.

"How do you know?"

"I found them on the security feed."

"How do you have access to the security feed at the liquor store?" I glanced at Tony. "Never mind." I walked up behind him. Both Bree and Coby were smiling as they paid for two bottles of wine. "Okay, so as of four-thirty they seemed to be buying wine for the evening. Its six-thirty now. We're supposed to meet at the restaurant in an hour. If they arrive and Brady and I aren't there, they'll wonder what's going on."

"Have you tried calling Bree's cell?" Tony asked.

"About a million times. It goes straight to voice mail."

"Maybe she just forgot to charge it."

I hoped that was the case, but the feeling of dread in my stomach told me otherwise.

"What if you and I show up at the restaurant? If they're there, we'll tell them Brady had an emergency and asked me to come along to round things out."

I looked down at my uniform. "I'll have to stop at home to change. We'll need to hurry."

"Just give me ten minutes to clean up."

I thought about the red dress I'd bought and decided against it. This wasn't the time to show up looking like a sex kitten, so I put on a dressy pantsuit and a pair of low heels. By the time we got to the restaurant it was five minutes to seven. Bree and Coby weren't there, so we got a table for four and waited. Every second that ticked by seemed like a lifetime. If they didn't show up, I didn't know what I'd do.

By seven-thirty I realized they weren't going to show. That terrified me more than I could find words to communicate. "What are we going to do? How will we find them?"

"I don't know." Tony tossed some money on the table even though we hadn't ordered anything. He took my hand and led me out into the frigid Montana night. After we'd climbed into his truck and he'd turned on the heater, he looked at me. "I know the fact that they didn't show looks bad, but we can't panic."

I rubbed my hands together in front of the heater vent. "Easier said than done."

"We need to keep our heads about us. Let's review what we know."

I took a breath and let it out. "Haven't we already done that? I feel like we keep going over the same thing, and at the end we're no better off than we were when we started."

"I don't disagree with you, but I've found that at times going over the same information more than once eventually leads to a flash of insight."

"Okay. Let's do it. You start."

Tony took a moment before he started to speak. "You first met Coby when you came across the accident he had with Armand Kowalski. Given that someone injected a drug into Kowalski's system, and Coby was the only other person there, chances are Coby intentionally caused the accident. He knew Kowalski had been watching him. One of them was literally behind the other on the road. Coby must have realized he'd been made and decided to get rid of the guy, so he caused the accident and injected the drug."

"And then he asked me to breakfast," I picked up the story. "He told me a wonderful tale about a son looking for his long-lost mother and I fell for it. We spent the next week running around town trying to get a lead on the woman he apparently just wanted to kidnap."

"Meanwhile," Tony continued, "Maria found out Coby was looking for her and decided to come to the United States to check things out. Her husband was out of town and she saw her opening but still had to bring her three bodyguards with her. Once they arrived, she managed to give them the slip. I guess we can assume she went to stay with a friend while she checked Coby out."

"Coby is here in White Eagle. If Maria knew that, it makes sense she would want to be close by, where she could get a look at Coby and decide for herself if he was telling the truth."

"Okay," Tony said. "Say she's here. Where would she be?"

"With Carl Willoughby."

"The teenager she knew when she was staying with Edith?"

"Yes. There was an age difference, but I suspect they were close. I found drawings in the sketchpad in Edith's attic similar to the ones Carl had in his home. They were of Maria. It looked like she must have posed for hours. And she gave him the pendant she'd been wearing when they met. If Edith was still alive, I'd suggest she went to her; Carl seems like the next likely choice."

"Okay. Let's go see Carl."

Chapter 15

When we arrived at Carl's house, the vehicle Coby had been driving was parked in front. We got out of the truck and slowly snuck up to a window. I couldn't see everything that was going on, but I could see Bree and Carl sitting on the sofa.

"It doesn't look like there's anything sinister going on," I whispered.

"There's nothing obvious, but look at their body language. There could be more going on than the scene would indicate. Maybe you should call Mike just in case there's a problem," Tony said softly in my ear.

I walked away from the window and made my call. I'd just hung up when I heard a shot. "Bree!" I ran as fast as I could to the front door. Tony tried to stop me, but he's big and I'm small; I slipped right past him. When I pulled open the door I found Bree on her knees and Carl on the floor. Coby turned to face me, which gave her the opportunity to kick him in the leg.

"What the…" Coby turned back to Bree. Tony took advantage of the diversion and hit Coby over the head with a bat he'd found propped up against the wall. He was out like a light.

"Are you okay?" I grabbed Bree and hugged her tight.

"I'm fine. Carl—"

"I called 911," Tony said, kneeling next to him. He placed his finger on his neck. "He has a pulse. Go find some clean towels. We need to stop the bleeding."

Bree ran down the hall for the towels while Tony found something to tie Coby up with and I placed the palm of my hand over Carl's gunshot wound and applied pressure. There was so much blood. Too much. Luckily, Mike arrived a few minutes after Bree returned with the towels and took over. It was at that point that Bree passed out cold.

Tony carried her to the sofa and I wet a towel for her head. When she came to, I asked her if she was all right.

Bree put her hand to her head. "I'm okay. Just a little dizzy."

She lifted her head and attempted to sit up. I used my weight to help her.

"How did you find us?" Bree asked. "I thought we were dead for sure."

"I tried to figure where Maria might have gone. The sketches Carl did of her when she stayed here as a young woman suggested a relationship closer than just casual acquaintances. The age difference was significant, so I'm not suggesting a romantic relationship, just a warm friendship. I took a shot that she might come here if she needed a place to hide. I guess Coby had the same idea."

"He said he had a feeling Carl was closer to his mother than he let on the first time he spoke to him. He wanted to do a follow-up interview. I had no idea what was really going on until we got here and Carl got all defensive. I know you won't believe it, but it's the man Coby works for who caused Maria to run in the first place, after an attempted kidnapping."

"Tony and I just found that out today." I looked to where the paramedics, who had just arrived, were working on Carl. "I hope he's going to be okay."

"Me too. He probably saved my life. Coby pointed the gun at me and threatened to kill me if Carl didn't tell him where Maria was. Carl insisted he didn't know, and I thought I was a goner, but then Carl jumped up and tried to get the gun. That's when he was shot."

By the time Mike had followed Carl in the ambulance, Frank had interviewed Bree, and we'd all been released to go home, at least two hours had passed. Bree was pretty shaken up, so we all headed over to my cabin for Valentine's Day frozen dinners.

"I wonder how Coby knew Carl and Maria were so close," I mused when we all settled down with our meals.

"Coby had the journals," Bree said. "I guess what he told us they said and what they really did were quite different. After reading them, he knew Maria had stayed in touch with Carl, so he assumed he'd know where she would be."

"*Did* Carl know where Maria is?" I asked.

"He said he didn't, but I don't know for sure," Bree answered. "I hope Maria's okay. It must be terrifying to have people after you."

"Maybe she'll be safe now that Coby has been arrested."

"Someone hired him," Tony pointed out. "I'm sure that same person can hire someone else. When you're as rich and powerful as Milovich, the people he loves are never completely safe."

Chapter 16

Saturday, February 17

"I'm really kind of nervous," I said to Bree as I picked imaginary lint off my black wool pants. "I don't know why I'm nervous, but I am."

"I know," Bree whispered back. "It almost feels like we're meeting royalty. I wonder what she's like."

"Don't overthink it. I'm sure she's a lot like everyone else," Tony added.

Tony, Bree, and I had been invited by Maria Milovich to visit her in the house where she'd been staying while she watched the drama surrounding Coby play out. After arriving in the United States and giving her bodyguards the slip, she went underground to watch him to see how things progressed. If there was one thing she'd learned as the wife of a rich, powerful man, it was not to trust anyone until you'd checked them out thoroughly. I felt bad for the woman. It must be hard to love a man others wanted to harm.

"I spoke to Carl this morning," Tony commented, I think to distract us so we'd relax a bit.

"How is he?" Bree asked.

"He'll be fine. It turns out, the bullet went straight through, producing a lot of blood but not damaging vital organs. He'll be laid up for a while, but he told me Danko Milovich contacted him, and not only had he arranged to pay all Carl's medical bills, he transferred a large sum of cash into his bank account as well."

"Wow; that was really nice of him," I responded. "And here I've been thinking of him as a monster all this time."

There was a noise at the far end of the hallway. I looked up as an extremely beautiful woman who I realized right away must be Maria walked into the room. I stood up, uncertain whether I should bow, curtsy, or offer a hand in greeting.

"Thank you for coming." Maria smiled, offering me her hand.

"Thank you for inviting us," I answered. "I know this must sound crazy, but after looking for you this past week and talking to people who knew you, I feel like we're almost friends."

"We *are* friends," Maria assured me. "I don't know how I can repay you for saving Carl from the man who was masquerading as my son. I would never have forgiven myself if he'd died because of my stupidity."

"You couldn't have known what would happen," Bree offered.

"On the contrary. After thirty-five years as Danko's wife, I should have known exactly what would happen. I was rash and I'm sorry. I'll be going back to Serbia this evening, but in the meantime, I've had a meal prepared for us. I hope you're hungry."

Bree looked downright pale, but Tony, who appeared confident and relaxed, took Maria by the elbow and indicated she should lead the way. I took Bree's hand in mine and followed them. Once we were seated, a waiter offered us a selection of beverages. I wanted to keep my wits about me, so I declined wine and accepted water.

"Would it be okay if I asked you a couple of questions?" I asked.

"You may ask. I'll answer whatever I can."

"I feel like I have a fairly good idea of what occurred thirty-four years ago, but there's one thing I'm not clear about. It seems you went directly home to your husband after giving birth to your child, but the information we uncovered suggested your husband continued to look for you for years after you disappeared."

"My husband didn't want the man who tried to kidnap me to know where I was, so he pretended to look for me when I was actually safe with him all along. Of course, that meant I couldn't be seen in public. Not ever. During those first few years I remained in my suite, with only my husband, my bodyguards, and my servants to keep me company."

"That sounds awful," I said. "Did you ever consider leaving your husband and returning to your life in the States?"

"Being Milovich's wife isn't easy, and I thought of running away and changing my name so I could have a normal life quite often. In the end, however, I love my husband and am willing to do what's necessary to remain in his life."

"Seems like a lot to give up," Bree said.

"Perhaps, but being married to Milovich was something I chose a long time ago, a choice I plan to honor."

The conversation paused when the server brought our first course. When we were alone again, I asked the question in the forefront of my mind. "I know this is none of my business, but have you reunited with your son?"

Maria smiled. "I have. As it turns out, he has a wonderful life here in the States. A life I don't intend to interfere with. We've spoken and will stay in touch, but no one will ever know he's Danko Milovich's son. There's no way I would ever do anything to put him or his family in danger."

"And you never had any other children?" Bree asked.

"Sadly, no. I'm afraid in the world in which I live, being the wife or child of a man such as Milovich makes you a weapon that can be used against him. I realized shortly after I married him that the world I'd chosen wasn't one I would ever want to bring a child into." Maria's smile faded for just a moment. "But no need to feel sorry for me. I live a full life and am very happy. My child might not be in my life, but where he goes, so goes my heart."

After lunch, Tony dropped Bree at her house and then drove toward my cabin.

"It's early," Tony said. "Do you want to do something? I have a new video game to test."

"Actually," I grinned, "I have a date with Brady. It's a rain check from Valentine's Day."

"I see."

"I'm pretty excited about it. When I spoke to him on Valentine's Day, it sounded like he was relieved we weren't going out, but he called me yesterday and said he was disappointed our dinner hadn't worked out and wanted to reschedule. I've been wanting to try out that new restaurant, plus I did buy that smoking-hot dress. It'd be a shame if I never got the chance to wear it."

"Yeah," Tony answered. "A shame."

I turned to look at Tony. He seemed genuinely disappointed I wasn't free. "Shaggy is back in town; I ran into him yesterday. If you're really in to trying out your new game, maybe he's free. He's a lot better player than I am, so you'll probably have more fun with him anyway."

Tony smiled as he pulled up outside my cabin. "I think Titan and I will just have a quiet night. I'm kind of tired. Have fun on your date."

I leaned over and kissed Tony on the cheek. "Thanks. I'll call you next week."

Up Next from Kathi Daley Books

Farewell to Felines

Chapter 1
Monday, March 12

The hollow is a mystical place located in the center of Madrona Island. Given the rocky cliffs that encircle the area, it's protected from the storms that ravage the shoreline. The hollow is uninhabited except for the cats who reside in the dark spaces within the rocks. One of the things I like best about the hollow are the whispers in the air. Most believe the sound is created by the wind echoing through the canyon, but I like to think the whispers are the cats, heralding my arrival.

"Do you hear them?" I asked Tansy as we hiked to the top of the bluff that overlooked the ocean in the distance.

"No. The cats are quiet and that worries me." Tansy has some sort of mystical power that's tied in with the magic surrounding the cats. She and her best friend, Bella, are rumored to be witches. Neither of them will confirm or deny their witchy status, but both women know things that can't be empirically explained. Tansy and I had decided to venture into the hollow after she had a premonition that the cats were unhappy and leaving the area for reasons she didn't understand.

"It's odd not to have seen a single cat by this point." I paused and looked around. "Should we continue?"

"What does your intuition tell you?"

While I don't have Tansy's powers, it does seem I've been tasked with the responsibility of working with the island's magical cats. It's not something I asked for, but I know deep in my soul that my role with the cats is tied to my destiny. "My intuition tells me we need to climb higher."

Tansy smiled and nodded for me to walk ahead of her on the narrow path. The trail was steep and covered in shale, making for a difficult and dangerous passage. I'm in pretty good shape, so I'm well equipped for a laborious hike, but I could sense a storm coming and was afraid it would arrive before Tansy and I would be able to make our way back down the trail and out of the hollow. Still, over time I've learned to trust her, so I continued, despite the risk. The trail narrowed as it wound steeply up the mountain. My legs burned as I struggled to keep my footing on the unstable ground.

"If your sense is that the cats are leaving the hollow, where are they going?" I asked. "We do live on an island, after all. It's not like they can venture very far."

"If the cats are intent on leaving they'll find a way."

I supposed Tansy was right. I knew one cat in particular who seemed to make his way between the islands with seemingly little difficulty. Of course, Ebenezer was a special cat who seemed almost human at times, but then again, all the cats I'd worked with were special in their own way.

Once we arrived at the summit, I paused to catch my breath and admire the view. The ocean looked dark and angry as the storm gathered just beyond the horizon. I listened once again, turning slightly so I was facing the sea. "My instinct tells me we should head inland, but a storm is coming and I'm not sure continuing is the best idea."

"Never doubt your instincts, Caitlin Hart."

I glanced back toward the narrow path. "I guess it couldn't hurt to go on for a bit. I'd hate to have come this far and not find out what's causing the disturbance." The detour was going to add time to our journey and I hoped it wasn't all for nothing. Usually it was Tansy who would lead the way while I followed. It felt somewhat unnatural for her to be walking behind me. I wondered if this wasn't some kind of a test to prove my worthiness to expand my role as guardian to the cats.

We had just started down the path when Tansy gasped. I stopped walking and turned around to find her holding a hand to her chest. Her long black hair blew in the wind, creating a vail of sorts that framed her pale face. "Are you okay?" I walked back the way I'd come until I was at her side.

"No. I don't think I am."

"Should we go back?"

Tansy shook her head. "I am certain we must continue."

"Are you in pain?" I didn't think going on with a sick witch was a good idea at all.

"It is the hollow that's sick. For magic to survive, a very specific balance must be maintained. I feel that balance has been altered."

I had no idea what Tansy was talking about, but a bit of color had returned to her normally pale complexion that made me feel better. "Are you sure you want to continue?"

"I'm sure."

I took a deep breath and turned back to the narrow path. "Okay. But let me know if you need to stop."

I walked down the trail slowly so as not to tax Tansy, but to be honest, the farther I traveled the more urgent was my desire to run. "There's a fork," I said after we'd been walking a while. "Both paths are narrow and both continue inland."

"Close your eyes and focus on the paths ahead of you," Tansy suggested.

I did as she instructed.

"Which path feels right to you?"

"The trail to the left," I said with a confidence I wasn't really feeling.

"All right. Then we will continue to the left."

I nodded and headed down that trail. I could feel Tansy walking behind me, but I could also sense her distress. I stopped and turned around. "I can go on alone if you want to wait for me here."

"No. We're close. Can you smell it?"

I took a deep breath and wrinkled my nose at the stench. "What is it?"

"The source of the disturbance. It won't be long now."

"Until what?" I had to ask. This whole thing was beginning to freak me out. After several years of witnessing some truly spectacular things, there's no way I'm going to try to argue that magic doesn't exist, but the idea that it depended on some sort of perfect balance was a bit hard to swallow.

"There." I turned around in time to see Tansy pointing to a small body of water in the distance.

After we'd traversed the distance between where we'd stood and the small pond, I looked down at the murky surface of the usually pristine blue water. "Something's wrong with the water. It smells awful. I think it's been contaminated."

Tansy frowned. "Yes, I'm afraid it has been tainted. I imagine the lack of clean water is the catalyst that is driving the cats away."

"How can we fix it?"

"I sense the tainted water is a symptom of a larger problem. The answers we seek will reveal themselves in the coming days. We've done what we can for now."

I turned and headed back in the direction from which we had come. As we neared the top of the path and the bluff, I heard thunder rumbling in the distance. I glanced out at the dark sea as we paused momentarily before continuing down the other side. The dark clouds had completely blocked the light the sun would have provided. I just hoped we'd make it back to the car before the worst of the storm hit.

"Do you think the cats will return if we can find the source of the contamination and fix it?"

"Perhaps."

The walk down from the summit was accomplished much more quickly than the trip up. When we arrived at my car I noticed a large brown cat with bright eyes and pointy ears sitting on the hood. "Am I to assume this cat will be leaving with us?"

"Apollo is here to help."

"With the water in the hollow?"

Tansy picked up the cat. She closed her eyes and whispered to it in a language I didn't understand. The cat meowed a couple of times, and Tansy opened her eyes. "I'm afraid Apollo is here to help you resolve a different issue. Follow his lead and you'll find the answers you seek."

"Has someone died?"

Tansy nodded but didn't answer. My heart sank. Occasionally, cats appeared to help me deal with a problem other than a murder, but most of the time when one of them appeared someone had died. I wondered who.

As we drove back to Pelican Bay, where Tansy lived with Bella, the sky continued to darken. The wind had picked up quite a bit, and I could tell by the heaviness of the clouds that we were in for a serious storm. I dropped Tansy at her house, then drove back toward the peninsula, where I lived. I was nearing the point where I turned on to the peninsula road when Apollo started meowing and jumping around the car. I slowed and eventually pulled over.

"What is it? Are you trying to tell me who's died?"

"Meow." Apollo began pawing at the glove box. I opened it, and a sheet of yellow paper fell out of it and onto the floor.

"That is just the program from Sunday services at St. Patrick's."

Apollo jumped from the front seat onto the floor. He picked the paper up in his mouth, then leaped back onto the seat. Once he was settled he placed the program on the seat between us.

"I don't understand what you want me to do. Today is Monday. Services are on Sundays.

"Meow." Apollo placed his paw on the program.

I looked at what he seemed to be pointing to. "That's the set list the adult choir sang during yesterday's service. Do you want me to go to St. Patrick's?"

The cat didn't respond.

I tried to figure out exactly what it was the cat was pointing to. "Do you want me to pay a visit to Father Bartholomew? Oh God, he isn't the one who died, is he?"

The cat still didn't respond.

"It isn't Sister Mary?" My heart began to race as the thought entered my mind. I'd known Sister Mary for most of my life. She was my best friend's biological mother and almost a member of my family. "Please tell me it isn't Sister Mary."

Apollo just stared. I'm not sure if cats can experience frustration, but I got the feeling this cat was quickly becoming impatient with me. It seemed his silence represented a negative response, so I continued to guess at what it was the cat was trying to tell me. "Maybe someone whose name is on the list?"

"Meow."

"Okay, good. Now we're getting somewhere." The first name on the list was Thea Blane, the new director of the adult choir. "Do you want me to pay a visit to Thea?"

"Meow."

"Is Thea the one who's died?"

"Meow."

I closed my eyes and offered a silent prayer. She and I hadn't been close, but I'd known her casually for quite a few years. She was single, lived alone, and didn't seem to have any family on the island. Still, I was sure there were those who would mourn her passing. I looked at the darkening sky. Thea lived all the way over in Harthaven and the storm was getting closer. If I continued to her place, we risked getting caught in it. "Are you sure Thea's the one we need to find?"

"Meow."

I glanced at the sky one last time. It would be a risk to make the trip, but I couldn't not go on the off chance Thea was still alive and Apollo's insistence was to save her, not simply to discover her remains. Making a decision, I pulled back onto the road and headed toward Harthaven.

When Apollo and I arrived at Thea's place I saw her car in the driveway. I still hoped she was alive and Apollo had brought us here for another reason. Once again, I prayed we weren't too late. I opened my door, which allowed Apollo to slip out of the car before I could stop him. I watched as he went to the door, then joined him on the front porch, rang the bell, and waited. My heart was pounding the entire time. I waited another minute before ringing the bell for a second time. When Thea still didn't answer, I knocked on the door and called out her name. When she still didn't answer I tried to turn the knob. The door was locked.

"Maybe I should call Finn," I said as the first raindrops began to fall. "Come to think of it, maybe that's what I should have done in the first place."

"Meow." Apollo hopped off the raised porch and ran around to the back of the house.

I pulled the hood of my sweatshirt over my hair and followed him as the rain increased in intensity. At the side of the house, I found the wooden gate leading to the backyard open slightly. Apollo slipped inside and out of sight. I felt I had no choice but to follow, so I lowered my head and trotted to the gate. When I reached the back door I saw it was ajar, and Apollo was nowhere in sight. I opened the door wider, calling to Thea as I did so.

I walked through the kitchen to the main living area of the house. "Thea," I called once again. "It's Caitlin Hart. Are you home?"

My words were met with silence. I looked around for the cat and spotted him sitting on top of a small desk against the wall near the foot of the stairs. When he saw I'd found him, the cat jumped down and ran up the stairs. As I followed, I heard the first rumbling of thunder in the distance.

At the top of the stairs was a short hallway that led to four rooms. The first contained a bed and a dresser and looked like a guest room. It appeared to be empty and undisturbed, so I continued to the second room, which turned out to be a bathroom. The third room looked a lot like one of the rooms in my Aunt Maggie's house that she used for a craft and sewing room, so I imagined the last door would lead to the master bedroom. When I saw a pair of feet sticking out from the far side of the bed I knew for certain what I had feared since Apollo had snuck into the house was true. Thea Blane was dead.

Recipes

Tortellini Chicken Soup—submitted by
Nancy Farris
Grannie's Potlicker Soup—submitted by
Taryn Lee
Mexican Potatoes—submitted by Janel Flynn
Turkey Cheese Baked Soup—submitted by
Marie Rice

Tortellini Chicken Soup

Submitted by Nancy Farris

One of my favorite quick weeknight meals. Add crusty bread and you have dinner!

12 oz. skinless, boneless chicken breasts, cut in 1/2" cubes (I've also used pork cut in strips)
6 cups chicken broth
½ cup sliced leek or chopped onion
1 tbs. grated fresh ginger
¼ tsp. saffron threads (optional)
Salt and pepper to taste
Dash of soy sauce to taste
1 9-oz. pkg. refrigerated tortellini
½ cup fresh baby spinach

Coat a large saucepan with olive oil. Heat, then add chicken and cook and stir for 3–4 minutes. Add broth, leek/onion, ginger, and saffron. Add salt, pepper, and soy sauce.

Bring to a boil. Add tortellini. Return to boiling, reduce heat, and cook according to instructions on tortellini package. Stir occasionally. Remove from heat. Ladle into bowls and top each bowl with some spinach.

Grannie's Potlicker Soup

Submitted by Taryn Lee

1 tbs. vegetable oil
3 cups smoked ham, chopped
1 large Vidalia onion (sweet onion)
2 cloves garlic, minced
8 cups chicken broth
1 16-oz. bag frozen collard greens
1 can black-eyed peas, drained and rinsed
1 28-oz. can diced tomatoes
Salt and pepper to taste

Heat oil in a large pot over medium heat. Add the ham along with the onions and cook until the onions turn clear. Add the garlic and cook for about 1–2 minutes more.

Add the broth, then bring to a boil. Stir in the frozen greens and bring back to a boil, then reduce heat and cover; simmer for 20 minutes.

Add the rinsed peas and tomatoes along with salt and pepper to taste. Cook for 15 more minutes and it's ready to serve. Corn bread is a great addition to go along with the soup.

Mexican Potatoes

Submitted by Janel Flynn

Boil 10–12 med. potatoes (Gold or Yukon work best, in my opinion). Cool, peel, and cut into slices.

Combine:
¾ cup onion, chopped
¾ cup green pepper, chopped
1 cup mayo
¾ cup milk
2 tsp. salt
1 tsp. pepper
1 cup American cheese (I like the Mexican cheese blend better)
¾ cup green olives and ripe black olives, mixed

Arrange in layers. Save ½ cup grated cheese to put on top. Bake at 375 degrees for 20–30 minutes.

Turkey Cheese Baked Soup

Submitted by Marie Rice

1 large white onion, finely chopped
2 lbs. cooked turkey meat
1 26-oz. can cream of chicken condensed soup
1 32-oz. carton low-sodium chicken or vegetable broth
½ tsp. black pepper
Dash or two of cayenne pepper
Dash or two of garlic powder (optional)
8 cups shredded cheddar cheese
Milled flaxseed (optional)

Sauté chopped onion in a 4-quart pot until cooked. Chop turkey meat into bite-size pieces and add to pot, along with all remaining ingredients except cheese and flaxseed. Warm over medium-high heat, stirring. Adjust seasonings as needed. Let cook for about 6 minutes once warmed up.

Preheat oven to 350 degrees.

Spray or butter a deep 9 x 13 casserole dish or an 11 x 15 oversize casserole baking dish. Ladle ⅔ of the turkey sauce into the casserole dish. Spread about ⅔ of the cheese over the sauce. Layer the remainder of the turkey sauce, then the remainder of the cheese. Add an optional sprinkling of milled flaxseed over the final cheese layer for a little crunch in the topping.

Bake for about 35 minutes. Allow to cool 10–15 minutes before serving.

Notes:
* I frequently put a 3-lb. turkey breast roast into a slow cooker throughout the year. Depending on how quickly our family goes through the turkey meat, sometimes I can get one of these soups cooked.
* Leftover turkey from Thanksgiving or Christmas are perfect to use in this recipe.
* Use any combination of white and/or dark turkey meat.
* Chopped onion can be placed into the 4-qt. pot without sautéing it, but the sauté action gives it greater flavor.
* I find soup mugs to be the best way to serve this soup, versus a soup/cereal bowl, because you can also warm your hands on it.

Books by Kathi Daley

Come for the murder, stay for the romance.

Zoe Donovan Cozy Mystery:

Halloween Hijinks
The Trouble With Turkeys
Christmas Crazy
Cupid's Curse
Big Bunny Bump-off
Beach Blanket Barbie
Maui Madness
Derby Divas
Haunted Hamlet
Turkeys, Tuxes, and Tabbies
Christmas Cozy
Alaskan Alliance
Matrimony Meltdown
Soul Surrender
Heavenly Honeymoon
Hopscotch Homicide
Ghostly Graveyard
Santa Sleuth
Shamrock Shenanigans
Kitten Kaboodle
Costume Catastrophe
Candy Cane Caper
Holiday Hangover
Easter Escapade
Camp Carter
Trick or Treason
Reindeer Roundup
Hippity Hoppity Homicide – *March 2018*

Zimmerman Academy The New Normal
Ashton Falls Cozy Cookbook

Tj Jensen Paradise Lake Mysteries by Henery Press:

Pumpkins in Paradise
Snowmen in Paradise
Bikinis in Paradise
Christmas in Paradise
Puppies in Paradise
Halloween in Paradise
Treasure in Paradise
Fireworks in Paradise
Beaches in Paradise – *July 2018*

Whales and Tails Cozy Mystery:

Romeow and Juliet
The Mad Catter
Grimm's Furry Tail
Much Ado About Felines
Legend of Tabby Hollow
Cat of Christmas Past
A Tale of Two Tabbies
The Great Catsby
Count Catula
The Cat of Christmas Present
A Winter's Tail
The Taming of the Tabby
Frankencat
The Cat of Christmas Future
Farewell to Felines – *March 2018*

Writers' Retreat Southern Seashore Mystery:
First Case
Second Look
Third Strike
Fourth Victim
Fifth Night
Sixth Cabin – *May 2018*

Rescue Alaska Paranormal Mystery:
Finding Justice
Finding Answers – *May 2018*

A Tess and Tilly Mystery:
The Christmas Letter
The Valentine Mystery
The Mother's Day Mishap – *April 2018*

Sand and Sea Hawaiian Mystery:
Murder at Dolphin Bay
Murder at Sunrise Beach
Murder at the Witching Hour
Murder at Christmas
Murder at Turtle Cove
Murder at Water's Edge
Murder at Midnight

Seacliff High Mystery:

The Secret
The Curse
The Relic
The Conspiracy
The Grudge
The Shadow
The Haunting

Haunting By The Sea

Homecoming By The Sea – *April 2018*

Road to Christmas Romance:

Road to Christmas Past

USA Today best-selling author Kathi Daley lives in beautiful Lake Tahoe with her husband Ken. When she isn't writing, she likes spending time hiking the miles of desolate trails surrounding her home. She has authored more than seventy-five books in eight series, including Zoe Donovan Cozy Mysteries, Whales and Tails Island Mysteries, Sand and Sea Hawaiian Mysteries, Tj Jensen Paradise Lake Series, Writers' Retreat Southern Seashore Mysteries, Rescue Alaska Paranormal Mysteries, and Seacliff High Teen Mysteries. Find out more about her books at **www.kathidaley.com**

Stay up to date:
Newsletter, *The Daley Weekly*
http://eepurl.com/NRPDf
Kathi Daley Blog – publishes each Friday
http://kathidaleyblog.com
Webpage – **www.kathidaley.com**
Facebook at Kathi Daley Books –
www.facebook.com/kathidaleybooks
Kathi Daley Books Group Page –
https://www.facebook.com/groups/569578823146850/
E-mail – **kathidaley@kathidaley.com**
Twitter at Kathi Daley@kathidaley –
https://twitter.com/kathidaley
Amazon Author Page –
https://www.amazon.com/author/kathidaley
BookBub –
https://www.bookbub.com/authors/kathi-daley
Pinterest – **http://www.pinterest.com/kathidaley/**

Made in the USA
Middletown, DE
30 January 2020